Theodore Johnson

The preaching of the cross

forty eight short meditations upon I.-The life of sacrifice, and II.-The atoning death,

for Lent, Holy Week, Good Friday and Easter-tide

Theodore Johnson

The preaching of the cross
forty eight short meditations upon I.-The life of sacrifice, and II.-The atoning death,
for Lent, Holy Week, Good Friday and Easter-tide

ISBN/EAN: 9783741193521

Manufactured in Europe, USA, Canada, Australia, Japa

Cover: Foto ©Andreas Hilbeck / pixelio.de

Manufactured and distributed by brebook publishing software
(www.brebook.com)

Theodore Johnson

The preaching of the cross

Preface.

ONE of the most striking proofs of the zeal and devotion of Churchmen and Churchwomen of the present time is the increased attendances at the Church's Services, and the marked interest taken by them in the full observance of Her Holy Days and Seasons.

Much has been done of late years by word and act towards the better keeping of Lent, Good Friday, and Easter. I trust this present effort may advance still further the holy practice of Meditation among Christians. Some there are by reason of bodily infirmity or weakness who may be unable to attend the public services at Church; while others, I pray, may be led to take up these Meditations each day in their times of private devotion, with an earnest desire to be " Apart with Jesus."

While the old, sweet truths remain unchanged, yet it will be found I trust helpful to surround them with some new thoughts and lessons in company with those culled from many existing manuals on the Passion of our dear Lord and its teaching.

Where known Authors have been made use of to any extent, I have been careful to name the work from which the quotation has been taken, so that I trust any omissions in this way may be pardoned if found herein.

Among those works to which I am much indebted for quotations during the compilation of the following meditations, I would mention: "Questions of Faith and Duty," by Bishop Thorold of Winchester; Goulburn's "Thoughts on Personal Religion," and "The Pursuit of

Holiness," Rivington; "The Attraction of the Cross," Rel. Tract Soc.; Gerhard's "Meditations," Parker; "Cruciana," by John Holland, Liverpool; "Practical Reflections on the Gospels," Rivington; "Meditations on the Suffering Life of our Lord," and "Nourishment of the Christian Soul," Trans. by Bp. Forbes; "The Daily Round," Whitaker; "The Cambridge Bible for Schools," R. Clay and Son; "Sermons on the Lord's Prayer," Rev. Brooke Lambert; Sermons by Rev. S. B. James, D.D.; "The Worship of Heaven," by Rev. Dr. Trinder; "Notes on Catechisings;" "A Lent Manual" and "Seven Last Words," by Rev. T. B. Dover; "The Sinless Sufferer," by Rev. W. Skeffington; "The Outstretched Hands," by Rev. A. Williamson; "The Mind of Jesus," by Rev. G. S. Gruggen; "Things New and Old," by John Spence, 1657; Brook's "Noah's Ark," 1662; Bishop Wilson's "Sacra Privata;" with those well-known Manuals of Devotion, "The Imitation of Christ," "The Christian Year," George Herbert's "Temple," Taylor's "Holy Living and Dying," etc., etc., also verses from several of the Hymnals used in our Churches.

In conclusion, I would add that these Meditations have not been the work of a few weeks, but rather they have been drawn from the Author's "Good Friday Addresses" and "Lenten Courses of Sermons," so that the whole of the Meditations have been delivered in this way during the past fourteen years.

The two series of Meditations may also be used as Addresses, viz., Part I. during Lent, Part II. on Good Friday, or they will be found suitable for Daily Readings at Lenten Services. To arrange for this use I have purposely placed them in this order.

"*Shirley,*" *Avenue Road,*
    South Norwood Park, S.E.

Introduction.

IF any Introduction be needed for this little volume, I would ask in the words of the saintly Thomas à Kempis, " Wilt thou, O disciple, learn to love Jesus with thy whole heart ? Wilt thou thoroughly purify thy soul from its stains, and enrich it with every kind of virtue ? Wilt thou gain glorious victories over the enemies of thy salvation, and receive abundant consolation in thy troubles and griefs ? Wilt thou make great progress in prayer, obtain final perseverance, die holily, and reign eternally in Heaven ? Then exercise thyself in continual meditation upon the Life and Death of our Divine Saviour."

It is indeed a blessed privilege to find ourselves " alone with God " during the solemn season of Lent. To look within to see ourselves as God sees us, and then, having pleaded for pardon for our past sins, to meditate further upon that Perfect Life—that Wondrous Death of Jesus, with the mysteries that crowd around it. In such a scene may we not truly be said *to lose self that we may find God ?*

In Prayer we learn to give ourselves, our souls and bodies, to God. In Meditation we learn to receive Him in return. As Prayer may be described to be " Converse with God," the creature speaking to the Creator, so Meditation or Mental Prayer is the Christian waiting, watching for, and reflecting upon God's answer. With the eye of faith we are able to contemplate God's presence, and so to feel our own unworthiness, and great need of Him.

The Father's Arms can alone bring pardon, peace, and rest to the weary prodigal seeking his long-lost Home.

It is necessary to true Meditation that we realize the Presence of God. There must be a " conscious speaking to a personal God," or but little good may attend our efforts. Again, in Meditation as in Prayer we must be definite. If we seek an audience of the King of Heaven, and He grants it, we must be ready to receive His message. And what is that message ? Is it not truly " The Story of the Cross " ? for " Nowhere is the true character of God so fully revealed as in the Cross." " The Cross was designed to be the most compendious and vivid expression of all religious truth. The testimony of Christ is the testimony of the Prince of Martyrs. Nowhere else does truth utter her voice with such distinctness, such fulness and emphasis. Were an Angel to descend from Heaven to become the teacher of men, his instructions might well be listened to with eager-ness. But the Cross is the Teacher of Angels. It is the Deity Himself bearing witness to His own doctrines. Every truth in the Bible brings us at last to the Cross, and the Cross carries us back to every truth in the Bible ; so that the sum and substance of all truth is most impressively proved, illustrated, and enforced, by ' Christ and Him Crucified.' " [1]

From the City of Mansoul to the Palace of God, the Highway bears five names. Mark the order as laid down in the Great Master's prayer :—

" Adoration," " Confession," " Petition," " Intercession," " Thanksgiving."

[1] " The Attraction of the Cross," pp. 24, 25 ; Rel. Tract Soc.

Have our poor prayers and meditations these definite marks of "The Pilgrim Way"? "We must go by the eternally ordained path of love to Him, Who is the Revelation of Eternal Love, and suffer His Love to charm us into kindred love. We must lay our hearts close beside His Heart, that they may learn to beat with the same motion."[1]

Therefore let us often call our thoughts and affections around the Cross. Let it ever be our refreshment and joy, for He "that liveth and was dead," and is "alive for evermore," hath said, "Because I live ye shall live also." [2] "Is it not a touching thought, that the Death was His and the life is ours; His the Sorrows, the Weeping—ours the relief, the smiles, the joy; His the Agony, the Shame, the Curse—ours the pardon, the honour, the glory, the immortality; His, too, the Restored Life, the Life that shall never die—ours to live and reign with Him for ever." *Amen.*

> " The Cross my all,
> My theme, my inspiration, and my crown!
> My strength in age, my rise in low estate!
> My soul's ambition, pleasure, wealth, my world!
> My light in darkness, and my life in death!
> My boast through time—bliss through eternity—
> Eternity too short to speak its praise!"

[1] Theodore T. Munger.
[2] Fr. "Attraction of the Cross," pp. 24, 344, Rel. Tract Society.

Index.

Part I.—Learn of Jesus How to Live.

ARRANGED AS
NINE ADDRESSES OR TWENTY-FIVE MEDITATIONS.

xiv.

Part II.—Learn of Jesus How to Die.

ARRANGED AS

ADDRESSES FOR THE THREE HOURS OR TWENTY
MEDITATIONS.

Additional.

The Preaching of the Cross.

PART I.

LEARN OF JESUS

HOW TO LIVE!

"SINGLE ACTS OF VIRTUE, WROUGHT BY THE GRACE OF GOD, ARE THE STEPS TO HEAVEN—WHETHER INWARD, OF PENITENCE, OR FAITH, OR HOPE, OR LOVE BREATHED FROM THE SOUL TO GOD, ... OR OUTWARD, OF SELF-DENYING LOVE, OR PEACEMAKING, OR ACTIVE SERVICE."
—*Anon.*

"SHEW ME THY WAYS, O LORD: TEACH ME THY PATHS."
—*Ps. xxv. 3.*

"MY SOUL IS ATHIRST FOR GOD."—*Ps. xlii. 2.*

THE MIND OF JESUS.

I.

" Let this mind be in you, which was also in Christ Jesus."—PHIL. II. 5.

HE Cross this season takes the place of the preacher. The Church's loving note of holy warning is *The Mind of Jesus*. "Let this mind be in you, which was also in Christ Jesus."[1]

We are led away from the world's cares for a short space. All the anxieties, toils, fascinations, and schemes of business, pleasure, or earthly care are laid aside, that we may be for a season "apart with Jesus," to study His Divine Will—to probe the thoughts of that pure Mind—to meditate upon the God-Man, your Saviour and mine. Oh! grand and noble ideal of perfect humanity, "the Son of God in His days of suffering and trial."

Even while the palms of victory wave around Him the Cross darkens the path of suffering to our Jesus. So we, in our brightest days, must expect the gathering of sorrow's clouds. It is God's Will to fit us for His Eternal Presence by the stern discipline of trial and suffering. It is enough for the disciple to be even as his Master.

To understand the depth and mystery of the story of Lent and Holy Week, it is necessary to try to view the scenes which crowd upon each other in rapid succession in the light of truth as Jesus saw them all. What conflicting

[1] Phil. ii. 5.

A

passions racked His pure soul and wounded His loving
heart! Let us consider them together.

Mark with holy reverence, O disciple, thy Master's hatred
of sin with its terrible penalty to be paid in those coming
hours of His Passion. No wonder we earnestly pray, " By
Thy Cross and Passion, Good Lord, deliver us!" We so
often hate sin only after our own wills, conditionally, for
certain secret sins we still cling to and cherish. We still
retain some secret love—some hidden desire, for the old evil
within, is still lurking as a deadly poison to kill the soul, while
outwardly we deign to raise the voice of censure, or point
with the finger of shame toward the more glaring evils of
others. And why so? It may be to stand well with our
fellows—to retain our good character. We thus deceive self,
and think we hide from God the evil within us, by indulging
in those little sins only. But let us reflect. What sin is
little in the sight of God? The tiny drops in that terrible
flood which bore off the sinless Jesus to a cruel death were
your little sins and mine. Learn then, of Jesus, during
this Holy Season, How to live! How to hate sin! " Let this
mind be in you, which was also in Christ Jesus,"[1] and so
may ye be led into the living way.

Again, shall we not meditate upon *The intense love of Jesus
for sinners.* The Passion of our dear Lord is so full of
mystery to erring mortals! Who can understand or fathom
the deep, strong, infinite love which reigned in the heart of
Jesus to lead Him to suffer and to die for us? Our love—
yours and mine—too often, alas! arises from selfish motives.
The self-sacrificing love of Jesus was perfect—*Perfect Love.*
He gave Himself to be " a full, perfect, and sufficient
Sacrifice, oblation, and satisfaction, for the sins of the

[1] Phil. ii. 5.

whole world." [1] No finite mind can fully grasp this truth. We can only marvel and adore Him for such an Offering.

The soul of man is immortal. No earthly object can satisfy it. Planted by God within us, it yearns for His Presence too often clouded and hidden from us by our sins.

The Royal Sufferer conquered evil by that all-absorbing love which wrung tears from His broken heart—tears of blood in Gethsemane, and streams of living water, a cleansing tide from Calvary. Nothing short of this could wash out the guilt of a sin-stained world.

Then, there was in the mind of the Holy Jesus *The foreknowledge of suffering.* He ever saw the bitter, cruel, stern conflict of the world's hatred steadily approaching Him on all sides,—surging around Him to overwhelm Him as in the flood of an angry sea. How mercifully God hides the future from us! How full of misery life would be—nay, would it not be intolerable, if we could but peer into the trials of to-morrow—the sorrows of next week—or the losses and failures of the coming year. What a keenness this foreknowledge must have given to the sword which pierced the soul of the sinless Jesus. The criminal awaiting death in his dreary cell, slowly counting out the sorrowful hours until judgment comes upon him, has indeed a hard lot. Yet, what is this compared to the sufferings of that pure soul—that cloudless life of patience and love—now meeting alone the last dread conflict with Satan, by which his evil rule must be overthrown for ever.

How can we fail to love Him in return for such an offering? Who can resist His tender appeal to the souls of men—" Behold, and see, if there be any sorrow like unto My sorrow ? " [2]

---

[1] Holy Communion Service.　　　　[2] Lam. i. 12.

Do we not desire to draw closer to our dear Lord at this holy season to show our love for such an offering! Like S. John, the beloved disciple, or the faithful Magdalene, we would remain in His Presence to learn His mind the better that we may be found faithful in the day of trial. " So God loved the world, that He gave His only-begotten Son, that whosoever believeth in Him should not perish, but have everlasting life."[1]

II.

" Christ also suffered for us, leaving us an example, that ye should follow His steps."—1 S. PETER II. 21.

E desire to follow in the steps of Jesus. We wish to make our life *Christ-like*. It is a noble ideal. How can we best set about it? His example stands out as a Beacon of Light and Love to guide us to Himself. How many passages are there wherein the Divine Light of that Pure Sinless Life flashes across our path! " Christ pleased not Himself "[2]—He was "Meek and lowly of heart "[3]—or again, "He made Himself of no reputation."[4]

How truly marvellous was the Humility of Jesus! In His moment of popularity while the glad Hosannas of the first Palm Sunday rent the air, His Royal Head was meekly bowed to receive the burden of those later cries of reviling and rejection, the combined scorn and hatred of a bitter multitude, raising the shout of " Crucify Him! Crucify Him!"[5]

[1] S. John iii. 16.   [2] Rom. xv. 3.   [3] S. Matt. xi. 29.
[4] Phil. ii. 3.   [5] S. Mark xv. 13.

We know by bitter experience how hard it is to be mis-understood by those we love. Think then of those wounded feelings of Jesus when He subjected Himself to that angry, disappointed mob who clamoured for His death—"Crucify Him: Crucify Him:" because they knew not that His Kingdom was not of this world. They misunder-stood His Divine Mission as the Saviour of their souls. Have we the mind of Jesus here? How keen are we to resent injury—to repel insult: We have a dignity to main-tain—a position to uphold: We stand on our rights: Pride asserts itself even to the injury of others—And, yet, Jesus teaches the better way:—"Take My yoke upon you, and learn of Me; for I am meek and lowly in heart: and ye shall find rest unto your souls."[1] May we walk along the path of Humility in close companionship with Him during the coming season.

"He humbled Himself and became obedient unto death, even the death of the Cross."[2] Here again is our example —our lesson of Humility. May we learn it faithfully. What strange words are these! At first they seem to jar upon our worldly ears: Unbelief doubts it—Pride mocks at it—The world sets it aside for a convenient season, which it well knows will never come ; while Love seeks the shadow of the Cross, and Faith gazes upon it, until the full light shines out from it. *The Mind of Jesus* appears. Its peace and power, truth and glory, spread as a halo around the faithful disciple's life until men may learn that "we too have been with Jesus."

"Obedience is a fruit that groweth only in the Garden of God."[3] When selfish indulgence and wilfulness crept into the Eden of old, it withered away, until the life-giving

[1] S. Matt. xi. 29.   [2] Phil. ii. 8.   [3] Anon.

streams from Calvary refreshed, renewed, restored it for grace and glory to lost mankind.

Christ's human nature rose towards its perfection, as the mind that was in Him led Him triumphant on the way of the Cross. He wills to bring us by a like, lowly, path to the same glorious end, even to abide in His presence for ever — Whereby we pray, " Through Jesus Christ our Lord," for through Him alone can we find peace and rest for our souls. " Neither is there salvation in any other."[1]

" O for a lowly, contrite heart, believing true, and clean,
    Which neither life nor death can part from Him who dwells within ;
    A heart in every thought renew'd, and full of love divine ;
    Perfect, and right, and pure and good : a copy, Lord of Thine." *Amen.*

Shall not our one petition be :—" Lord, what wilt Thou have me to do ? "[2] How will the Master answer us ? Will He not surely say, " Take up thy cross daily."[3] " Learn of ME, for I am meek and lowly of spirit."[4] " Seek ye first the Kingdom of God and His righteousness, and all these things shall be added unto you."[5] " Let your light so shine before men, that they may see your good works, and glorify your Father which is in Heaven."[6]

Even so Lord—" Thy Will be done."[7]

[1] Acts iv. 12.   [2] Acts ix. 6.   [3] S. Luke ix. 23.   [4] S. Matt. xi. 29.
    [5] S. Matt. vi. 33.   [6] S. Matt. v. 16.   [7] S. Matt. vi. 10.

THE LIFE OF RETIREMENT.

I.

"Jesus went up into a mountain apart to pray. And when the evening was come, He was there alone."—S. MATT. XIV. 23.

THE Holy Season of Lent has been called "*The Springtide of God.*" It is also man's sowing time. New rules of life, new aspirations, new resolves have not only to be made, but they must be kept. It is a solemn season of reparation, so that it is meet for us to retire from the world with its many changes and pleasures—its busy occupations—to find our God in prayer and meditation—to learn some new lessons in the School of Jesus for our future guidance. His perfect manhood, assailed by temptation, is a noble lesson for each one of us, to teach us to conquer through Him. "We have no power of ourselves to help ourselves."[1]

Let us think about Jesus in His retirement. How often during His seasons of glory or triumph, as well as in His times of trial and disappointment, He practised this going "apart to pray." These holy seasons were indeed true aids to strengthen Him in His dread battle against the powers of evil.

Although there is but a scanty narrative recording our Blessed Lord's personal doings in the Gospel Story, yet this going apart to pray, is mentioned on seven different occasions, and these do not include that hidden life of purity in childhood, or the sacred seclusion of His youth and early manhood, spent at Nazareth, in which He so wonderfully prepared Himself for His ministry.

[1] Coll. II. Sun. in Lent.

May we not picture the Saviour Child retiring to some lonely spot near to the village home and workshop, where the grassy slopes frequently bore the impress of His knees. Here for a little time He would leave home, mother, and companions to talk to His Father in Heaven. Then as years passed on, and the child had grown into a youth, or youth was leading up to manhood, may we not again see Him, so real, so true, so pure, so faithful, so unlike His companions, often seeking this spiritual retirement. Shall we not follow the Master here, and try to be more regular—more methodical—and more strict in our times of devotion. These must not just be a few moments snatched from the world of toil, or pleasure, but there must be a definite system in our times of meditation and prayer. Public prayer, and open acts of worship, will not excuse us from acts of private devotion. We must learn of Jesus to be more in earnest, less spasmodic in the time we devote to communing with our God. Surely there is much to make good in your life and mine here.

Let us glance at these seasons of retirement as we find them recorded in the Gospel Story—Let us go apart with Jesus into the wilderness, ere the words of His Beloved Father are scarcely uttered, " This is My Beloved Son, in Whom I am well pleased."[1] " Then was Jesus," in His hour of glory, " led up of the Spirit into the wilderness to be tempted of the devil."[2] He, Who was unknown among men, yet worshipped and adored by angel hosts, went apart to pray—to suffer—to be tempted—to conquer the Evil One during the great forty days fast.

What a preparation for meeting Satan ! The Body subdued—the Will trained—and the Soul quickened and strengthened, by daily private intercourse with the Father.

[1] S. Matt. iii. 17.   [2] S. Matt. iv. 1.

May we, too, not gain spiritual strength, by withdrawing a little from the world—a few minutes daily for extra Bible reading, during this solemn season—A little more time for prayer and meditation—More frequent Church-goings and communion—Some definite rule made which shall enable us to offer to God "ourselves, our souls, and bodies to His service."

Again, the Divine Master visited the solemn silence of the mountain region, before He called His chosen ones, His twelve disciples. It was a great event in His earthly ministry and He marked it as such by this withdrawal from the world to pray apart.

Those chosen companions who were to witness His miracles of power, whereby sin, disease and suffering became obedient to His Word—Those fellow workers with Him, ordained, set apart by Him to be the pillars and foundation stones of His living, spiritual Church. It was no light undertaking to call each one separately from the fishing boat, or world of toil, that they might dedicate themselves to God as fellow labourers with His dear Son, in setting up His Spiritual Kingdom upon earth. For their sakes, therefore, the Saviour prayed in secret. He pleaded with His Father alone to endue them with spiritual power from on high, that they might faithfully unto death perform the work of Apostles and preachers of the Gospel Story to lost souls.

Oh! that we, too, may learn to seek grace and guidance in undertaking new work—To take our plans and schemes to Jesus that He may bless them, and strengthen us to perform them aright to the glory of God and the benefit of our fellow men. Oh! that we may always dedicate our choice of companions to Him, Who, by "going apart to pray" gives us this simple lesson. There would be fewer failures in life, less unhappy unions, if we could but learn this lesson in the school of Jesus.

II.

"I have prayed for thee, that thy faith fail not."—S. LUKE XXII. 32.

"Wherefore He is able also to save them to the uttermost that come unto God by Him, seeing He ever liveth to make intercession for them."—HEB. VII. 25.

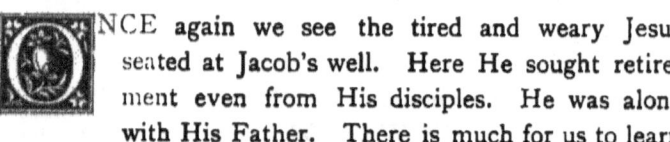NCE again we see the tired and weary Jesus seated at Jacob's well. Here He sought retirement even from His disciples. He was alone with His Father. There is much for us to learn here. In times of devout thought, when we are "*Alone with God*"—when the great truths of salvation seem to rivet our attention, then we are constrained by the Holy Spirit of power to love more—to desire more—to learn more that Divine Mystery, " In Christ we see God is Love."

The whole secret of that Perfect Life, that wondrous Death, is made plain to us, and the message it reveals is, " Thou art Mine, O child of My heart. For thou hast wandered, yet not beyond the bounds of My Love. Turn thee unto ME again. I have still need of thee. Thou art indeed precious unto ME." "Wherever I meet '*thou*' and '*thee*' in the Bible, it seems as though it spoke to me alone, and sometimes it comes home to me with wondrous power. Even now in reading this text, I can feel, as it were, some friendly, Fatherly Eyes upon me, a gentle Voice speaking to me— such looks and such words as this weary world cannot give —and I can feel in my heart a conviction that whether I do love God, or whether I do not love Him, the Saviour still says to me, as tenderly as if He were not holy and I not sinful, ' Thou shalt love.' "[1]

These beautiful words seem to explain the Life of Retirement. Is it not well for us to leave those we love for a season, that we may cling the closer to our God, for there is truly a great danger of our earthly surroundings weaning away some of our affection from Him.

Once more see how Jesus was interrupted by that poor sin-laden woman at Sychar, who came near to draw water. Hear how lovingly He unfolded her past life of evil. He put His finger upon her sin. None who draw near to the Saviour for aid are sent away unhelped, unless they reject His teaching or oppose His Will.

We see here the unselfish nature of Jesus; we learn also that time, strength and talents used for the good of others are also used for God.

Yet another scene opens up before us. Again physical weakness has asserted itself, and Jesus being weary seeks rest and retirement beyond the Sea of Galilee. How these failures in our dear Lord's bodily strength endear Him to us—Do not these proclaim Him to be Perfect Man—touched with our infirmities, yet without sin. What a bond of unity we have with our Elder Brother here!

His fame was at its height. Men flocked from all parts to His presence, and thus it was the seclusion of the wilderness was broken by the multitudes who followed Him to hear His words and witness His works of healing. Shall we then murmur if the world or friends interrupt us in our times of withdrawal from them. If duty breaks in " *It is the voice of God.*" We must obey—Jesus did so—and then

[1] From Sermons and Lectures by Rev. S. B. James, D.D.

returned to His seclusion after the multitudes were fed, lest
they should make Him a king by popular clamour. " His
Kingdom was not of this world."[1]   He was so misunderstood. In the solitude of the mountain He received strength
to go forth on the morrow to break down this worldly spirit
of popularity by hard mysterious sayings, which when men
heard, we read: " From that time many of His disciples
went back, and walked no more with Him."[2]   How different
His character and conduct to ours? We who court praise and
renown from men: we who live to be extolled, made much of :
we who value so highly popular favour, and deeply grieve if
we are by chance passed over, or so quickly envy those who
may be preferred, even by right, before us.   We surely need
more retirement with Jesus, ere we learn the right way.

The two last occasions when our dear Lord went
apart to pray were that night of prayer preceding the
glorious dawn of the Transfiguration morn, and that sacred
scene of Gethsemane—where He as a willing Sufferer
taught us to overcome all hindrances, and to pray, " Not as
I wilt, but as Thou wilt—Thy Will be done."[3]

We too may remember how the Apostles were rewarded by
their retirement to the Upper Chamber at Jerusalem after
their Master's Ascension into Heaven, for there He vouchsafed to pour out His Spirit of power upon them to enable
them to carry out His last commands.

To all lives *Retirement is a blessing*, therefore, we should
ofttimes practise it for our soul's sake. Let us open the
life's page, this Lent, " Alone with God :" Let us mark
well the tale of omissions and wanderings : Let us weep
bitter tears of penitence over the marred life of sinful
disobedience. Once that page was a fair one and truly

[1] S. John xviii. 36.   [2] S. John vi. 66.   [3] S. Matt. vi. 10.

beautiful to behold : even now, blurred as it is, God's Eye is ever upon it, although we may seldom care to look back into the past. Yes, the Master waits for our return to Him—Oh, may we answer :—

> " Then let my life be given, my years for Thee be spent ;
> World-fetters all be riven, and joy with sorrow blent ;
> Thou gavest Thyself for me, I give myself to Thee."[1]

THE LIFE OF UNION.

I.

" In Him was Life ; and the Life was the Light of men."
—S. JOHN I. 4.
" In Him we live, and move, and have our being."—ACTS XVII. 28.

THERE are certain questions that come to us in our quiet sober times of meditation, when we try to shut out the world with its flood of cares and trials, and find ourselves alone with God. In these holy moments of calm the Evil One is aroused to battle with us in secret. Many and varied are the means he employs to secure our downfall, and probably one of the most subtle of these is by tempting us *to Doubt*.

Satan always suits his temptations to our particular tastes or natures. He studies keenly our likes and dislikes until he in his subtilty so weaves his deadly meshes around us that we fall. Oh ! the power of that terrible word " Doubt." Look at the man or woman who begins life with Doubt as a companion. How soon it becomes a part of themselves. They live or rather exist in a very atmosphere of Doubt. First, it may be, under the false pretence that it is a seeking

[1] Miss Havergal.

for more knowledge. " Something deeper " is necessary for the very satisfying of their souls—the cravings of their restless minds—until Doubt, nourished and fed by such natures, springs up and surrounds them blotting out all that is fair and beautiful in Life: nay, even at length shutting God out from that Life until it becomes a burden too heavy indeed to be borne.

It is a true picture, however sad it be represented, the Doubt as to the existence of a God, followed by the doubt as to their duty to that God. This brings about the cruel state of despair in some lives. Such an one looks up to Heaven, and says, " Perhaps." He is led to explain it all away by argument, or logical deduction. The great problem of Life with the relations between God and man boldly standing out as a clear proof of Faith, while Love, Hope, Trust and Peace, meet him everywhere. He cannot understand, or explain it, so he thrusts it aside, afraid to encounter the truth. All around becomes if not darkness, a sickening gloom, until Doubt drowns the soul in despair and the cry goes forth, " There is nothing to live for." All is doubtful, false, dark, uncertain. No wonder he asks in despair, " Is Life worth living ? "

Let us not doubt, for doubt implies Ignorance rather than Unbelief. To doubt God is to acknowledge with shame that we know Him not. Rather shall we flee to the presence of the Great Teacher Jesus, Who still says : " Learn of ME, that ye may find rest unto your souls."[1]

Never be led to Doubt because you are not able to understand. We move in such a small circle. Our existence and powers are so cramped, our knowledge so finite. We know so little, yet those mysteries which so baffle us, are God's

[1] S. Matt. xi. 29.

mercies sent to draw out our Faith in Him. What can you give me in place of my God ? asks the earnest Believer of the Infidel.   There can be no doubt about the Life, Work, Sufferings and Death of God's dear Son—our Jesus. These things are facts in History.   There can surely then be no doubt about God the Father's Love in sending the Saviour to live and to die for us; or, again, of the sanctifying grace and presence of the Holy Spirit within us, given in obedience to the promise of that Saviour.

It is all so beautifully simple, and yet so deep. The finite and limited understanding is, at once, overcome by the keener sight and nobler gift of Faith until the clouds and mist of doubt lift from the weary soul, and the Life of Jesus becomes our Light Eternal. " In Him was Life ; and the Life was the Light of men."

II.

"In Him we live, and move, and have our being."—ACTS XVII. 28.

S Life worth living ?   Life so varied, so chequered and full of change. Life with its varied states and conditions, with its many spheres of existence that we describe them under the simple titles of " Spiritual," " Natural," " Social," " Business," or " Home Life "; without perhaps attaching much importance to what these words really imply in all their fulness. They are each distinct, complete and real—yet each represent in a marked way its many changes and chances; its bright days of sunlight side by side with its nights of shadow ; its moments of trial, failure and victory opposed to its times of sorrow,

and its seasons of joy.   There is truly so much in Life that
we are apt to cry out : Who may explain it ?

Life is indefinable.   It is not the creature of Scientific
Electricity, but it is the existence of God within us.
Implanted by God, Life must be offered and dedicated to
God, that it may be received and accepted by God when
its mission is fulfilled.

The most perfect Life of the God Man, Jesus, made
its offering complete in those last death cries from Calvary,
" It is finished : "[1] " Father, into Thy Hands I commend
My Spirit."[2] Oh, that we may be able to make this offering
ere we pass into the greater mysteries of Eternity.

Then, again, we use the word " Life " for the little world
we occupy comprising our every thought, word and deed.   It
is peculiarly ours.   What value is there in it ? Of what does it
consist ? How are we using this immortal God-given talent?

There is, first, " The Visible Life : " what a man appears
to be.   Then follows " The Hidden Life : " what a man really
is before God.   It is such a delicate, difficult question, yet
how good for us to meet it, to think it all out, during this
Lenten season.

Here then, we find summed up the whole state of man,
whether spiritual, mental, or temporal : so we must look
within to understand aright.   We must go to the source to
find the motive, pure and true ! Too often, alas, we lose
ourselves, our object in life, by reason of overlooking it—by
looking out into the world ; by scanning the lives of others,
instead of looking within to seek for God in the Life of the
soul.   A penitent of old found this alone to be the best
way, and it still stands true.   Within read :—Know thyself
to be immortal—A mystery—" The Child of God ; " the

<hr>

[1] S. John xix. 30.   [2] S. Luke xxiii. 46.

possessor of a living soul in which He condescends to dwell in thee that thou mayest be His alone. Nothing can ever satisfy the human soul but God's presence. Therefore the answer to "Is Life worth living?" comes to us in the silent whisper of the conscience. "In Him we live, and move, and have our being."[1] Life is worth living when God is in us, with us, for us, and through us to help others. We are *made* as sons and daughters; *redeemed* as disciples and brothers; and *sanctified* as living servants to love, to serve, and to magnify Him for ever.

To begin with the Spiritual Life : we may ask reverently, and humbly, Why was I created? To worship—to work—to complete God's grand scheme of creation upon earth—to be His representative below; thus it is we stand at the head of His great family of all created beings. The mighty message "Let Us make man,"[2] by which the first pure souls were called into Life and being, was again re-echoed in tones of mercy, "Let Us save man," ere the Father of Love sent the Redeemer to live The Life of Salvation to a lost race. Yet once more in tender whispering accents the promise of the Comforter fell from the lips of Jesus, as a Guide and a protection from evil for the future life of service to His faithful disciples.

Spiritual Life, then, is a Reality as much as Natural Life. Do we understand this? We are by nature so indifferent and careless about all things spiritual. Is it that we feel so helpless here? Do we need a Leader to point the way? A Pattern to follow? A Guide to awaken zeal, and to give courage against any perils we may encounter on the road? To whom can we go? Even to Jesus, Who alone is the "Author and Finisher of our Faith."[3] In His

[1] Acts xvii. 28.   [2] Gen. i. 26.   [3] Heb. xii. 2.

B

Perfect Life on earth we see a picture, *nay, the reality*, of perfect humanity; not beyond us, but One of us—One with us—not out of our reach, but a suffering Brother; a Burden-Bearer of the sins of others—even ours, yours and mine. How pure, how noble, how faithful He appears —conquering all by His perfect obedience. As we stand in awe and wonder meditating on that holy, spotless life of trial and suffering, we may read the answer that Life is worth living.

III.

"Saved by His Life."—ROMANS V. 10.

ESUS, your Jesus and mine—Who alone knows the Father's Heart—Who alone hath obeyed His Will and fulfilled His purpose—He would teach us that "Life is of God." Man was made to receive Light from God. By type and prophecy, by personal intercourse or vision, we learn this truth in the Old Testament. By revelation, face to face with the God Man, the same lesson is given in the New Testament. Nothing has been left undone on God's part to perfect our Salvation.

Sin plunged man in darkness, doubt and despair. Slowly, though surely, it blotted out man's Maker, duty, and home; while it ushered in those grim attendants, sorrow, suffering, and death as its wages and burdens to be grievously borne. It needed the Light of God's presence in Jesus to dispel the shadows of evil: it needed the sad story of that pure suffering Life of Love to bring Life and Light to souls steeped in sin. In a worldly sense, it is no wonder that men reject the Lord of Life. His self-sacrifice is so unlike all earthly things—so full of mystery. Yet while none may probe that mystery, all must be led to believe, to adore, to follow that Life even unto Death, that crowning marvel of Love and self-abasement. The taunting Infidel points with scorn at the Crucifix, saying, "His game is played out;" while the faithful believer answers, Oh! not so! thanks be to God! His Death is not *The End*, but *The Beginning of the New Life*—It is not the dropping of the curtain at the finish of earth's Life and Hope, but it is the flinging open of the gates of the higher and more glorious Life, through which alone floods the Light of Salvation upon the souls of men. We have an Easter story, followed by an Ascensiontide sequel. And now, He Who died that we might live, "ever liveth to make intercession for us."[1]

Truly we serve a Living Jesus, not a dead Christ. Let us learn then this Lenten season in our meditations upon His suffering Life and Death, that :—

(a) "So God loved the world"[2] by giving His Eternal Son to live the pattern life for lost—lost mankind.

(b) So God still loves us by imparting His Holy Spirit to us in Holy Baptism, according to the parting promise of Jesus—"that whosoever believeth in Him" (that is in Jesus) "should not perish, but have everlasting life."[3]

Mark the changed life of the Apostles after the gift of Pentecost. Jesus was not now *with* them—but *in* them—by the presence of His Spirit. So we believe this grand truth of "every one that is born of the Spirit."[4] Truly "the power from on high hath overshadowed us."[5] Born

[1] Heb. vii. 21.   [2] S. John iii. 16.   [3] S. John iii. 16.
[4] S. John iii. 8.   [5] S. Luke i. 35.

again in Holy Baptism we live renewed as " Members
of Christ, Children of God, and Inheritors of the Kingdom
of Heaven."

Dedicated from our earliest years to our Master's service,
"We live unto Him and not unto the world," ever winning
a victory by Faith and submission to His Divine Will. The
powerful shafts of evil fall harmless around us as day by
day we are nourished by the power of the Spirit within,
and supported by His ever abiding presence.

" Sun of my soul, Thou Saviour dear, It is not night if Thou be near:
   O may no earth-born cloud arise To hide Thee from Thy servant's
      eyes." [1]

So shall the inward temptations be overcome, mastered,
cast out, until by thought, word and deed we proclaim to
others that we have been with Jesus.

True Life reveals the power of the Spirit directing,
guiding all, until " self-will " gives place to " self-sacrifice."
It is " enough for the disciple that he be as His Master." [2]
" For as many as are led by the Spirit of God, they are the
sons of God." [3] Is Life worth living? Yes! For " in
Him we live, and move, and have our being." [4]

   " Lord! I am dead, and Thou art Life—revive me.
   Justice condemns: let mercy, Lord, reprieve me." *Amen*.

[1] A. & M., 24, v. 1.   [2] S. Matt. x. 25.   [3] Rom. viii. 14.   [4] Acts xvii. 28.

IV.

COMPANIONSHIP.

"For me to live is Christ."—PHIL. I. 21.

"Lord. make me to know mine end, and the measure of my days, what it is; that I may know [1] how frail I am."—Ps. xxxix. 4.

 PENITENT of olden time thus laid his petition before his God and Father of Mercy. It was a posting up of the ledger of life with that Saint of other days. He earnestly desired to " know himself" better, even as God knew and saw him in the past and present, that he might the better plan the future in the service of his Master.

If we turn to another scene we find the Divine Master Himself weeping as He beholds the past, present, and future of Jerusalem on His triumphant march to victory through suffering and death. He, " the fore-knowing Sufferer," felt a pang of sorrow for this wilful rejection of His Love. What is revealed in your life and mine when the Saviour's Eye is turned upon us? The city of Man Soul is still precious to God.

How many questions arise to perplex the earnest, anxious soul in its strivings after holiness! Why was I born? What is my mission?—my life?—the end and aim of my existence here below? We must go back to the beginning to enquire with reverence concerning God's purpose in sending us here. The answer then arises clear and simple. Because He had need of me—even poor weak, helpless, sinful me—to labour for Him, to love Him, to live in Him. Union with Him is stamped upon my very existence here.

[1] What time I have here.

It forms my chief claim and gives my best support. And
yet I am so unlike Him in all I think, and do, and say.
Why is this so? Because I am not fulfilling my object in
life. I am not fully performing my allotted work. Duty
neglected and a wilful serving of self proclaims how imper-
fectly I have kept my Baptismal vows as His child.

I am so vague and indefinite in all my spiritual aims,
hopes, desires and work. I choose to live alone, a stranger
to His Divine Will and purpose. Yet He still loves me
with an everlasting love : an unchangeable and constant
love follows me still in my waywardness, though humanly
speaking, *which I feel can never be,* I just weary and tire Him
out by this want of response, this loss of union.

> " ' Lord, Thou hast here Thy ninety and nine; are they not enough for
>   Thee ? '
> But the Shepherd made answer : ' This of Mine has wandered away
>   from ME ;
> And although the road be rough and steep, I go to the desert to find
>   My sheep.' "

Next, how am I filling this station to which I have been
called, with its many responsibilities and privileges? Make
me to know it, Lord!

God never makes ends—objects, without creating means
to attain them. There is always a ladder let down from
Heaven to aid His children to climb there, so He hath
endued us with intelligence—the mystery and power of
knowledge : Hence I have power to choose the good and
to avoid the evil. Do I use it aright ?

The five senses, those mysterious powers which place me at
the head of all created beings are they not bonds of union
given by God that I may know, and love, and magnify, and
worship Him the better. How encouraging all this is.

In the present, as in the past, He still leads me on.
" Nearer, my God, to Thee : Nearer to Thee."

My needs He knows, and supplies even lavishly, readily
and constantly, without fail to make the way easy—plain
that leads to Himself. The hindrances and difficulties I meet
with are too often placed there by self, when in a moment
of weakness I have lent myself to the Evil One in the dark
hour of temptation. Jesus, thy Lord and mine, claims us
" Now," not hereafter only. He claims us first by virtue of
a Father's love. He claims us also by the seal of Salvation
for hath He not redeemed us—bought us—with a price.
The sacrifice of Himself as " The Lamb of God, which
taketh away the sin of the world."[1]

The power to know this truth has been implanted by
God. God's work within me is perfect. The end and aim
of knowledge is " Union." What a sweet thought and
refreshment to my soul in weariness and waiting here below.

Consider further how many and varied are the means our
God uses to draw us to Himself. Trouble, sorrow, sickness
or loss ; are not these often God's mark upon the Home, or
the Life ? It is only in the hour of Weakness that we can
cry—" Father, strengthen me." It is only in the time of
Sorrow that we can pray—" Jesu, comfort me." It is only
when Darkness comes upon us that we are led to plead—
" Sweet Spirit, enlighten me." Hence trouble, sorrow, sickness, or loss reveals God and our " Union with Him." Our
very helplessness proclaims us to be dependent upon Him.
Our very trials and troubles call forth His sympathy and
aid. Our object has been found, for the Lord is at hand
to bless and support us as His own children.

Yet " mine end " is not here. It will not be all smooth

[1] S. John i. 29.

travelling.   There are still battles to fight and to win for
God.   There are difficulties to contend with and to conquer.
The old enemies, Doubt, Despair, and Dismay, will arise
to prove our worthiness, zeal, and steadfastness.   Thus we
leave the future in God's hands, content to rest secure upon
His mercy.   United with Him " we stand," safely guarded,
secure from evil.   Alone, "we fall to rise no more."   Whether
through cloud or sunshine God calls us to Himself, ours is
to obey, to press on.   Whatever trials arise, " Underneath
are the everlasting arms "[1] to support us, and the end
remains, " Union with God ! "

> " There let my way appear steps unto Heaven,
> All that Thou sendest me in mercy given;
> Angels to beckon me, Nearer, my God, to Thee,
> Nearer to Thee."   *Amen.*[2]

THE LIFE OF SERVICE.

I.

" His servants shall serve Him."—REV. XXII. 3.

IT is commonly asserted that men and women
experience some difficulty in believing and
accepting the truth that God is with them
in their acts of daily toil, the trivial round, the
commonplace duties of life.   A doubt then arises, Is God's
presence a reality?   Then follows the temptation that
" Religion is religion " and " Business is business."   There
can be no blending here.   Each must be kept separate,
distinct, the one from the other.   God can have no place

---

[1] Deut. xxxiii. 27.   [2] Cardinal Newman.

in my daily toil, my household labours, my office, or work-shop. Let us pause here, and ask one solemn question, Why not ? Where is the scene of thy labours where God cannot enter ? This fatal thought would cut thee off from God, Who gives thee Life, and all things ; and would teach thee to live two distinct lives, one for self—another for God, as though Body and Soul did not form " One Man."

We have seen that Life is worth living only when God is in it brightening the path of duty ; leavening all our thoughts, words, and actions ; feeling for our disappoint-ments, failures and sorrows, directing when perplexed, leading us upward and onward through trial and difficulty, and accepting us when finished. Let us " cast all *our* care upon Him, for He *alone* careth for *us*."[1] The burden of Life will be the sweeter and less irksome if we receive it from His Hand in full Faith and sure Hope as His gift of Love :— " *The true Life of Service.*"

The sixth word of Blessing falling from the Master's lips declares, " Blessed are the pure in heart ; for they shall see God."[2] This purity of heart is the motive power to true Service, for " where your treasure is there will your heart be also."[3] The Life and Death of Self-sacrifice illumined with its bright rays a dark world, lost and shrouded in sin, to teach the power of a Life of Service ; and still there remain nineteenth century flashes, however feeble, before men, yet rich in value before God, as the golden crown of Duty en-circles the brow of the lesser Martyr and Witness to that Light. Such an one, surely, had learned her lesson well, when standing faithfully to her post, she, but a maiden of tender years, nobly braved death in order to send the dread telegraph message of the approaching flood to her

[1] 1 S. Pet. v. 7.   [2] S. Matt. v. 8.   [3] S. Matt. vi. 21.

unconscious neighbours living lower down the valley, that by her act of self-sacrifice they might still have time to flee for safety ere the waters reached them.[1]

"His servants shall serve Him." These simple words are taken from the last chapter in the Bible. What a grand sequel to all that is contained therein. There we may read about S. John's Vision of Heaven, your home and mine, with the River of Life "proceeding out of the Throne of God and of the Lamb;" with the Tree of Life, whose leaves are for healing of the nations; with the Light of God's eternal presence there. "And they shall see His Face;" and "His Name shall be in their foreheads."[2]

Here then is the reward for the Life of Service. Here is our goal—our prize for fighting the good fight of faith; for running the course below as true servants and faithful disciples.

II.

"Therefore are they before the Throne of God, and serve Him day and night in His Temple, and He that sitteth on the Throne shall dwell among them."—REV. VII. 15.

E too often speak of Heaven in a commonplace manner as though it were our sure possession whatever we may do or say here, yet God teaches otherwise. Commonsense and earthly judgment declare also against it. Only the tried soldier bears the medal here : only the faithful saint shall wear the crown hereafter. The Life of Service must precede the Life of Glory. The more tired the pilgrim here, the sweeter the rest hereafter ; the

---

[1] American Floods Incident.   [2] Rev. xxii. 5.

more weary the wanderer on earth, the brighter the joy in
Heaven. The victory is ours for Christ is with us in the toil
and strife, yet our part remains to "Work out our own salvation with fear and trembling."[1] It is not God's way that we
should cry, "Saved," and believe, " 'Tis done." No! or
what need of that pure, suffering Life of Jesus to point out
the way : Ours it is to follow on along that upward path of
toil as true disciples. Though it be the way of the Cross, yet
the Master's feet have passed on before us—His sacred footprints mark the track. There are no short cuts to Heaven.
It must ever be the old old way after Jesus worn by saints
of every age which leads us Home to God.

In God's great kingdoms, both Natural and Spiritual, the
time of probation is the preparation for power and reward.
We sometimes forget this, and in our better moments fall
into the other extreme, acting and living as though we were
all Soul and no Body. Yet the Body belongs to God. He
demands from it service, work, homage, and devotion.

Our Service is to leave God's mark on the world; to
influence Society *(our little world of acquaintances)* for
good; to make others the better for our example in the
parish or home circle.

We are apt to mistake our vocation in Life because the
world is so attractive ; pleasure is so engrossing, so alluring,
or business demands so much from us, that we feel there
is but little time for Religion, which we commonly name
the higher Service. This is surely a placing of Self first ;
a consulting of our own wills and inclinations, rather than
praying, "Thy Will be done," and really meaning it. If
we are in earnest, we must live Religion rather than wear
it as a cloke to hide self-interest from our neighbour's sight.

[1] Phil. ii. 12.

Life must be one unbroken act of worship if we are really worthy of the Name and Sign we bear as " Children of God, Members of Christ, and Inheritors of His Kingdom."

What is manliness ? What alone reveals those more tender graces of true womanhood ?   Surely it is the hidden nature declaring the true Image of God here and shining out from within us.   The pure Light of the Holy Spirit so illuminating the whole Life and Character, that we are led to admire the Dignity, the Virtue, the Upright Dealing, or the Holy Influence seen therein.   Truly hath it been said : " The Service of God improves upon acquaintance, gives more than it promises, and after a little effort is nothing but rewards, and rewards which endure for evermore."[1]

In the Life of Service the bottom round of Heaven's Ladder we have seen to be " Self-sacrifice," then follows " Humility," which estimates Self aright, and nourishes care for others.   Thus round by round, by Discipline and Daily Prayer, we mount to higher virtues, until, like Jacob of old, we are surrounded by the Heavenly Messengers who accompany us until God's Face appears to welcome us, and the weary sounds of toil are lost in the sweet words of welcome, " Well done, thou good and faithful servant ; . . . . enter thou into the joy of thy Lord."[2]

[1] Rev. F. W. Faber.   [2] S. Matt. xxv. 21, 23.

III.

"If any man serve Me, let him follow Me; and where I am, there shall also My servant be."—S. JOHN XII. 26.

IF men would accept the Life of Service as True Sons of God, how changed would this world become!

The busy Nineteenth Century Christian finds it no easy task to give this Life of Service. There are so many doubts to overcome caused by religious controversy; so much difference in practice of worship. Men are ever seeking to serve God their own way in preference to His way. They too often will only accept what they like in spiritual matters. Man's tastes too often are placed before God's glory. Again, there is too much sensation in religion; too much gossip about holy things in a spirit far from reverent; while on the other hand there is too little meditation, or even less daily communing with God.

To ensure our spiritual health, God must hold the chief place in our daily life. "Give admittance to Christ, and deny entrance to all others," quaintly writes S. Thomas à Kempis. Let us do nothing, go to no place where He cannot be present. Invite Him by prayer into the home circle, the place of business, or the workshop. His presence will bring a blessing to our labours; upright dealing and integrity to our schemes. Still the Master knocks. Why do we keep Him so long a stranger? It hath been said, "There is no handle without thy soul's door." Can it be that it remains barred by self-will from within? He Who once was a daily visitor to the carpenter's shop at Nazareth, Who called His chosen disciples from the receipt of custom or the fishing boats of Galilee, can never despise our labours. He still desires to be with us at all times, to draw out all that is noble, pure, and manly in thy life and mine.

Earth is still the training school for Heaven. Here below, in the world's busy market-places and workshops of toil, we must serve our apprenticeship for the Life of the world to come.

Idleness is a sin, and therefore it cannot be but repulsive to God's sight, and a hindrance to God's work. Let us pray against it in the words of the Collect for the Thirteenth Sunday after Trinity : " Grant, O Lord, that we may so faithfully serve Thee in this life, that we fail not finally to attain Thy Heavenly promises; through Jesus Christ our Lord.   Amen."

> " Take my life, and let it be
> Consecrated, Lord, to Thee." [1]

THE LIFE OF SUCCOUR.

I.

PROTECTION.

"Thou art my God ; my times are in Thy Hand."—Ps. XXXI. 14, 15.

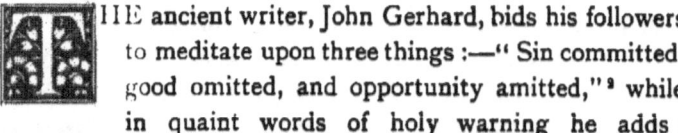

THE ancient writer, John Gerhard, bids his followers to meditate upon three things :—" Sin committed, good omitted, and opportunity amitted," [2] while in quaint words of holy warning he adds : " Remember, Three things are there above thee, the thought of which ever hold fast in thy memory; an Eye

---

[1] Frances R. Havergal.   [2] "Amissum," lost.

that seeth all things ; an Ear that heareth all things ; and
a Book in which all things are written."

In some such spirit, surely, the holy Psalmist dwelt upon
the ever-abiding presence of God. This presence was a
reality with him—a very quickening to his soul. Not only
did he realize God before to guide him—God behind to
protect and shield him, but God with him in the trial to
nerve his arm in the strife, to plan his actions in the time
of need, and to control his will throughout.

Thus confidence—sure trust—begets hope, and gives
power in the day of trial. What a truly blessed thought
it is to be able to claim the Almighty Father, Saviour and
Sanctifier as our portion here and hereafter. Not only that
we are His children, disciples and servants, but that He in
all His fulness, love and power is our " Emmanuel—God
with us."

All we are—all we have, or do, or say, must proclaim
Him. This is a solemn subject, " *My Times*." All the
weary years and the fleeting moments as they pass along,
bringing the Weal and Woe of Life. All the Sunlight and
Shadow of our earthly pilgrimage. All the Conquests and
Failures marshalled in wonderful order under the heads
of past, present and future. All those holy times of devotion and those horrible moments of sin—all are marked by
our God. How entirely, then, are we in His Hand.

We see here the other side of the picture from the Life
of the Body known to us as Human, Business, Social or
Home Life. Here the Light of the Divine Life breaks in
upon us. It may be that only the nobler souls grasp this
in full reality, yet nevertheless it is true to all, consciously
or unconsciously, we belong to God—we are all creatures
of His Love—we still remain children of His Grace. Here

a Temptation creeps in. We wonder if this is really true.
We begin to doubt whether the Infinite and All-powerful
God can stoop to take into consideration the little paltry
moments, the petty cares and worries, the trivial trials,
deeds and fragments of my poor worthless life.

Yes! because He alone is Infinite. A finite king can
only at the best know, feel for or help but a few of his
subjects. God is Infinite, and all things, however small
or humble, are known to Him. He Who taught that, Not
a sparrow shall "fall on the ground without your Father,"
adds, " But the very hairs of your head are all numbered.
Fear ye not therefore, ye are of more value than many
sparrows." [1]

With God the greatest heroes we read of are but as tiny
powers before Him, yet what comfort to feel assured that
the humblest, poorest Christian cannot act apart from His
All-seeing Eye. Our very unworthiness makes us the
more prominent in His sight. In our weakness we are
highly exalted before Him.

How beautiful this came out in the Life of Jesus on
earth. His teaching; His words; " Consider the lilies; " [2]
" If God so clothe the grass of the field; " [3] " Behold the
fowls of the air," [4] and other similar passages remind us
of God's tender and unceasing Care for us.

The Divine Master found time to care for the narrow-
minded Nicodemus with his strange prejudices in those
nightly seekings for truth. Again, those individual cases
of suffering each of which found an answering throb in His
great Heart of Love. Remember S. Peter's warning and
that tender look upon the fallen One which won him back to
penitence and tears. The dying Jesus found time in the

[1] S. Matt. x. 29-31.   [2] S. Matt. vi. 28.   [3] S. Matt. vi. 30.   [4] S. Matt. vi. 26.

agony of death to soothe the last hours of the penitent thief. Even Judas the traitor was tenderly dealt with : Nearly a year before His betrayal He warned His disciples of the traitor, yet at last the word went forth, "Friend, wherefore art thou come ? "[1]

Will then my Saviour not care for me ? Shall I seek His presence in vain during this Holy Season of Watching and Prayer ? No, this cannot be. The Hands that were once spread out to embrace me in all my shortcomings and waywardness will never be folded against me unless I refuse to accept His aid. The Heart that bled for me on Calvary's tree still loves me and yearns to win me back from evil.

"Though my sins against me cried, Thou didst clear me ;
And, alone, when they replied, Thou didst hear me."[2]

II.

"Thou art my portion, O Lord : I have said that I would keep Thy words."—Ps. cxix. 57.

MY Times have been fore-ordained of God, so they depend upon :—

1. *My Physical Strength.* 2. *My Opportunities.*

Firstly, we may consider what is revealed through my Physical Strength. As years pass on one by one of the delicate tissues and the vital powers of this frail body cease to act. Are not these things warnings that " My Times are well-nigh spent."

We rightly expect suffering as age advances, yet few

[1] S. Matt. xxvi. 50.   [2] " Praise," from George Herbert's " The Church."

understand this when the young die. Yet, strange truth,
there are more death-beds under forty than over. We
say, Ah ! yes; cut down before their time ! Not so ! Man
hath an appointed time to die, as he hath an appointed
time to live. Jesus died at thirty-three. He in His last
moments was able to say, " Father, into Thy Hands I
commend My Spirit."[1] Could we offer so willingly of this
sort ?

It is surely wrong then to murmur against early death.
Some of the greatest lives have been but short ones. Let
us rather in the true spirit of resignation pray with David,
" Lord, let me know mine end, and the number of my days :
that I may be certified how long I have to live."[2] Let us
make a better use of Life that we may learn to be more
resigned when Death comes. For what have we to fear if
God be with us. If God be our portion, whether we live
or die we are the Lord's.[3]

> " Lord, let my soul Thy goodness always see,
> And with strong confidence lay hold on Thee ;
> Prepared to kiss the sceptre or the rod,
> While God is seen in all, and all in God." *Anon.*

Then again, *My Opportunities.* With Jesus to see an
Opportunity was to seize it, and to make good use of it.

What a sad record of neglect here ! What blanks,
omissions, carelessness and wanderings ! There is still great
need to cry for mercy, for " all things are naked and opened
unto the eyes of Him with Whom we have to do."[4] " Thou
art my God: My Times are in Thy Hand."[5]

My Opportunities suggest a new start in things Spiritual.
New Resolutions in the present to be acted out in the

[1] S. Luke xxiii. 46.   [2] Ps. xxxix. 4, *P. B. Ver.*   [3] Rom. xiv. 8.
[4] Heb. iv. 13.   [5] Ps. xxxi. 14, 15.

future. Reparation for past evil to be made. How shall I begin? There is much to learn, and we must follow the Divine Master's Example in Gethsemane. There must be a submissive kneeling for grace that strength may be given to bear trial patiently and to do work perfectly.

Time is a sacred thing, yet how often it is frittered away. Fraught with golden opportunities on its swift wings we too often discover, alas! when too late, what we might have done. Remorse is a poor salve for Conscience's wounds. Let us therefore be watchful, ever ready to seize the present opportunity in God's Name for God's Glory and Service.

To do this we must not labour, or wait in our own strength. We must give a portion of each day to our God, as our special Present (offering) to Him. We must give more time to Prayer. The day must begin, continue, and end with Prayer. The soul must ever be trained to soar heavenward like the lark to tell its needs and extol its Maker beyond the dull, commonplace atmosphere of earth. There must be more systematic and regular Bible reading and Meditation. Times of Devotion are sweet moments spent in the Companionship of God. There must be more frequent Communions : a stronger craving for His very Presence : a keener hunger of the soul : more regular and faithful Church going : a higher standard of duty in which self is thrust back until forgotten.

Be patient, beloved pilgrim of the night, the watching may be a weariness now, yet pray on : the storm clouds may gather, yet the Master's face is not hidden for long ; Thy frail bark may totter and roll upon the vast deep, yet " underneath are the Everlasting Arms."[1] Thy God is with

[1] Deut. xxxiii. 27.

thee. Thy Times are in His Hand. Pray on—" In all
time of our tribulation ; in all time of our wealth : in the
hour of death and in the Day of Judgment : Good Lord
deliver us." Amen.

THE LIFE OF TOIL.

I.

" I must work the works of Him that sent Me, while it is day ; the
night cometh, when no man can work."—S. JOHN IX. 4.

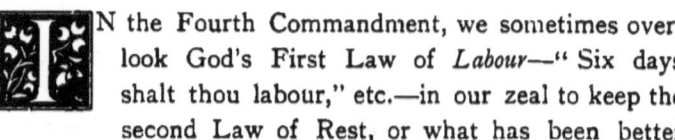

IN the Fourth Commandment, we sometimes over-
look God's First Law of *Labour*—" Six days
shalt thou labour," etc.—in our zeal to keep the
second Law of Rest, or what has been better
named " Worship." In Worship, the powers of the mind,
heart, and body, in short, the whole man, spiritual, mental
and natural, is turned from the earthly that it may be drawn
and directed only to the heavenly. In the Church's Holy
Seasons and Sabbaths the lull from earthly toil must not be
made indulgence or dissipation. The idle gratifying of the
human will or appetites must be carefully guarded against.
All admit that the weekly Sabbath of rest from labour
is necessary for the welfare of mankind, and the success of
his work below, because it brings with it a regaining of
strength, power and vitality. Wasted energy and worn
enthusiasm require repose. Both man and beast are the
better able to perform their allotted round of labour and
duty, for the Great Creator's Command that toil should be
suspended one day in seven. Yet we have no license for
indulgence here :—" I must rest from sin on the Church's
Holy Days : I must give up as far as possible all worldly

works and cares : so all earthly gain and toil suspended that
I may seek God's glory and my own salvation with all my
might." [1]

God's work is perfect, so at the Creation it was crowned
with Rest. Our work is imperfect, hence follows unrest,
dissatisfaction, impatience. Whenever we attempt to upset
God's great laws there must be " Failure." God makes
known His Will that it may be done, as we pray in the
Lord's Prayer. He offers grace to be used, not refused, or
abused, that is used wrongly. Therefore it is sin to resist
grace given for any end. It is sin to work evil when in the
same strength we might work good. If then it be sin to
fall, it is sin also not to rise. The slothful servant is
wicked. The unused talent was taken away. So God
teaches, for in Jesus Christ He hath given to the world a
mighty lesson against idleness. God made and redeemed
us to live useful, helpful lives. Not merely to shun the
evil, but to do the good. The passive state is not enough
here. As a son, a servant, a soldier, a member of His
Holy Catholic Church, I must be active, up and doing. I
am given great things to do for God in my Life and in the
world around me. I have knowledge and grace freely
bestowed upon me. God will then assuredly require an
account of my stewardship. I sin, if in any way I make
vain the life from God in me.

> " Lord, give the zeal and give the might
> For Thee to toil, for Thee to fight."

Then again, " My Work " for God—for others—for self—
What about that ? I have an allotted time to do it in, be
it long or short. What long life could offer to God the

[1] Heygate's Manual : IV. Comt.

Offering of Jesus? "It is finished."[1] I fear I cannot :
Mine is so imperfect, so ragged, and done in patches, with
threads missing; yet though it be blurred and stained, yet
it is still "My Work," and it cannot be done by others
for me.

We are so careless —We are not conscientious enough
over our work. It is often not our best and yet we dare
to offer it as such. The great sculptor, Michael Angelo,
was reproached for spending so much time over the angel-
figure he was carving to surmount the Cathedral spire of
his native city. His critics deemed it to be so far removed
from the eye of man that small imperfections need not be
perfected, but the master simply continued his work, saying,
" God and the Angels will see it."

Our work should present a full, perfect and sufficient
offering of ourselves, our souls, and bodies, to our God.
Our work may sometimes be mean or unpalatable, yet it
can never be degrading if done in the right spirit. It may
be, that this special work contains the particular Cross we
need to form *Character*. It may be, we lack the virtue
underlying this one Task. Our lives as a rule are so
commonplace—so uneventful. Let us not forget that God
made them. We too often mar them by attempting to do
other work not bearing His Name, or Approval. It may be
well each night to enquire on our knees, " What have I
done for my God to-day ? "

1 S. John xix. 30.

II.

"Whatsoever thy hand findeth to do, do it with thy might : for there is no work, nor device, nor knowledge, nor wisdom, in the grave whither thou goest."—ECCLES. IX. 10.

MAN has been given by God a body for work and a soul for prayer. The body is unable to work properly unless the soul prays aright. Therefore the Life of Toil is a Life of Prayer.

In what does the chief exercise of man's faculties consist ? 1. *Knowledge.* 2. *Love and Devotion.* 3. *Work.* To know, to love, and to do are primary symbols in the alphabet of Heaven. In the lowest sense it makes life brighter, of more value, to feel that our work is not all so much waste or loss of time in God's sight. Again, the very structure and mechanism of the body proclaims "Work." God's dear Son we have seen was a Man of Toil. As the curse of the first Adam was "In the sweat of thy face shalt thou eat bread,"[1] so Jesus, the Second Adam, sancti- fied human labour in His Life of Daily Toil. He removed the curse, and blessed the labour of our hands, for labour was not created by sin : It existed before the Fall. We read, "And the Lord God took the man, and put him into the Garden of Eden to dress it and to keep it."[2] All things are full of labour. In the Heaven above, the ministering angels fulfil with ready obedience their appointed tasks. All creation above, beneath and around us is busy. Learn then that toil is no curse, "except we labour without God." Then all avails nothing. Life is vain, and work is profitless. There can be no degradation in real, true, honest labour. It need not separate us from God or make us worldly-minded. We should

[1] Gen. iii. 19.   [2] Gen. ii. 15.

take our daily tasks joyfully, willingly even as the angels take theirs from God alone, and when completed we should again return to Him, to place the issue in His Hands. So in true faith and humility each cross-bearer following in the steps of his Divine Master must continually say, " I must work the works of Him that sent me, while it is day : the night cometh when no man can work."[1]

These words imply the *Necessity of Work :* Labour for God in obedience to His Divine Command. Our duty is not surely to question or to set aside, but to obey. The allotted task be it great or small has been given by God. Therefore His work carries with it a full assurance of power also bestowed to perform it fully and faithfully. Again the time is short. There is but a certain time to labour for each soul. " While it is day." So the Master teaches. Oh ! that sad record of wasted years, idle hours, which bear no impress of God's work. When night's deep shadows gently fall around us and the Angel of Death summons us to the Great Unseen, then all toil must cease. The tired labourer rejoices to lay aside his tools. The rest and brightness of God's presence, first in Paradise, and finally in Heaven, causes him to be glad rather than to fear the future.

How wonderfully this desire to labour was seen in the earthly life of Jesus ! In His childlike innocence He wondered at man's ignorance of toil. The first recorded words spoken by the Holy Child showed this in a marvellous manner. " How is it that ye sought Me? Wist ye not that I must be about My Father's business?"[2] Here was a mighty fulfilling of the prophecy of the Psalmist, " Lo, I come : in the volume of the book it is written of Me, I delight to do Thy Will, O My God."[3] The anxious and sorrowful parents did not

[1] S. John ix. 4.   [2] S. Luke ii. 49.   [3] Ps. xl 7.

realise the full beauty and truth of this searching question. That Mother, who rejoiced so truly in the finding of her Lost Child, only fully knew the meaning of these words, when the death-cry of the Saviour had proclaimed with power from Calvary's Cross, " It is finished." Finished— perfected—not only man's salvation, but that unbroken life of self-sacrifice, obedience and toil. Truly may we learn from Jesus that there can be no true rest without labour.

> " Thou, Who in the village workshop,
>   Fashioning the yoke and plough,
>   Didst eat bread by daily labour,
>   Succour them that labour now." *Anon.*

III.

" No servant can serve two masters."—S. LUKE XVI. 13, *R.V.*

E cannot be our own masters. The world with its passing delights seeks to rival God and rule our lives. We must not, then, serve the world, but rather make it serve us, using it under our Father's eye."[1]

Jesus, our Master, taught this lesson on the Mount of Temptation. That stern command, " Get thee hence, Satan,"[2] utterly discomfited and put to flight the Evil One. We too have this power to resist the Devil when assailed by him to leave the service of God for the service of another, be it the world, the flesh, or himself. Do we do this ? Do we not rather hesitate or complain by way of compromise, I have so little time for worship. The world or business is so exacting, and engrosses so much of my time that I am

[1] Daily Round, 316.   [2] S. Matt. iv. 10.

much too busy. Is not this a common excuse pleaded it may
be even conscientiously against times and acts of worship ?
What is the answer ? To be busy is the best preparation
for that worship. Our Blessed Lord did not call idle persons
to be His disciples. It was from the fishing boat or the
receipt of custom ; from the scenes of hard bodily toil, or
the world's busy mart, that our Divine Master sought His
chosen labourers to minister to the souls of men. A great
labourer has said, " My experience has taught me that
there is not any necessary connection between a life of toil
and a life of wretchedness," and another has declared, " To
labour is to pray," while we often make use of the old
proverb, " Heaven helps those who help themselves."

A modern book, " Self-Help," brings out the dignity and
nobleness of Labour. England's power and greatness has
not arisen from her conquests by land or sea. No! the
patient industry of her people has stamped their name on
the world's history. Her workshops, where toiling men
and women, yea and little children, labour on in dogged
perseverance and subtle skill ; These have made England
great by a perfect combination of work from Heart, Head
and Hand.

S. Paul in exhorting all men to be " not slothful in
business," adds but " serving the Lord."[1] A golden precept
for all to remind us that in the anxiety of the earthly toil
there still remains the Service of the Lord. Let us not be
slothful, careless, indifferent, in our daily duties to God, to
others, or to self. Let the busy round of daily toil proclaim
our life to be godly, righteous and sober. Let all be
perfectly regulated, lest softness creep in. Let no element
be wanting, or it will reveal at the last missing threads, a

[1] Rom. xii. 11.

broken and marred offering, which cannot be accepted as our final present to our Father in Heaven.

If it be true that " Idleness " brings want, misery and sin here, so it is true in the higher life of the soul. We may not, nay we *dare* not sever the unchangeable laws which bind the two in one being. The Wedding Garment must be woven on earth before it can be worn in Heaven.

Your work and mine here below, done in the Great Master's Name through grace given, is our only claim to the Rest above. The fig tree was cursed because it bore no fruit. What about ourselves ? In the Day of the Lord when earthly toil shall cease, " One shall be taken and another left."[1] Two souls ; Two lives knit together, united as one here —two who have lived, and loved, and laboured side by side, sharing the same home, meeting with the same friends, having the same outward advantages — occupation and honour among men, yet by God's just decree there will be strange separations, strange divisions at that dread time. Who is able to speak of these things ?

IV.

" Work out your own salvation with fear and trembling."—PHIL. II. 12.

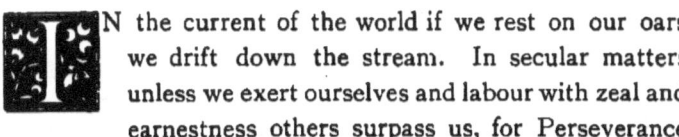

IN the current of the world if we rest on our oars we drift down the stream. In secular matters. unless we exert ourselves and labour with zeal and earnestness others surpass us, for Perseverance is the Watchword of Success. And so with things Spiritual. There must be no standing still in the Heavenly race : A host of bad desires, and evil habits are ever pursuing us like

[1] S. Luke xvii. 34, 35, 36.

the Egyptians followed Israel of old, and though the Red Sea
of trial and difficulty may stretch out before us ; yet our God
commands, "Speak unto the Children of Israel, that they
' *go forward.*' "[1]

A fish, the ancient type of a Christian, always sets its
head against the stream. If it turns it is carried down
with the fast-flowing current. To go forward implies toil—
perseverance—an object in view, and faith to win it. Do
not be dismayed if the task be a difficult one. With your
renewed efforts, Satan will also be more active to oppose
you, to mar your labours, therefore S. Paul's warning is
the more necessary during such a solemn season as Lent
when by increased devotion and more constant labouring
for God the powers of evil will arise in terrible force to
thrust you back to the old life of sloth or indifference—to
crush out the new-born energy that incites you to spiritual
exercises.

There is much in the Bible about "Work," and this
important word is often united to another, "Salvation."
Do we not remember the tender words of exhortation of
S. Paul to the Early Christians at Philippi. "Wherefore,
my beloved, as ye have always obeyed, not as in my presence
only, but now much more in my absence, work out your
own salvation with fear and trembling."[2] True fatherly
words of hope and comfort does the aged Apostle speak here
to us. As in 2 Cor. iv. 17, the saint's "light affliction,"
passing as a moment, "works out for him a weight of glory,"
so here his watchful, loving, reverent consistency, for his
Lord's sake, "works out," that is issues in the result of his
"salvation."[3]

Will our work tend to make us nobler, better, wiser men ?

---

[1] Exod. xiv. 15.   [2] Phil. ii. 12.   [3] Camb. Bible for Schools. Phil. ii. 12.

Will it make us more useful—helpful to our companions ?
Are we daily learning that we may teach others all those
sacred duties of the higher life ?   These are solemn questions for each soul to answer.   Your work and mine may be
hidden—silent—looked over—unnoticed by the world—yet
we may remember that there will be hidden saints in the Kingdom of Heaven.   Truly it is a noble work to silently—
quietly subdue the evil within, that good may the brighter
shine out.   Many lighthouses surround this sea-girt Isle as
warnings of hidden dangers and safeguards against evil.
Let each one ask, Am I a lighthouse for God ?   In the
Glory Roll of Nations, how strongly and brightly the great
lives shine out.   Yet the little lives are useful.   God hath
need of them, even yours and mine, insignificant—worthless,
though they may be.

We must remember that noble lives have no limit of useful-
ness.   They bring blessings to those who live them, and to
all who may be guided by their influence or example they lead
to Life Eternal.   A truly Christian life of labour—a faithful
doing of duty is a perpetual sermon to all.   It reaches the
most heedless and indifferent ; it arouses the slothful ; it often
sends the arrow of conviction to the idle heart.   The
simple village folk in Cornwall tell us that S. Leven's
pathway is always green because that holy man daily
passed along it to prayer and labour.   What story will our
life's pathway declare ?

Patience ; Strive on, O weary one ! for God is not un-
righteous that He will forget the Work done in His Name.

" O way Divine, through gloom and strife Bring us Thy Father's
    Face to see ;
  O Heavenly Truth, O Precious Life, Lead us through Toil to
    Rest in Thee." *Amen.*

THE LIFE OF TRIAL.

I.

"Take My yoke upon you and learn of Me . . . . and ye shall find
rest unto your souls. For My yoke is easy and My burden is light."
—S. MATT. XI. 29, 30.

PROBABLY the most powerful Meditation brought
forth by these words of the Saviour has taken
the form of a world-renowned picture, called
"The Vale of Tears."   It is truly a marvellous
and striking picture-sermon, painted under that subtle
influence of power that men call "skill," but shall we not
rather place it under the higher title of "Inspiration"? It
is God speaking through the artist in his last great work,
"*The Vale of Tears.*"

The dark valley of earthly sorrow, toil, and misery is
lighted up by the glorified figure of Jesus beckoning on
the varied and sin-stricken groups of sufferers with His
upraised Hand of Love, while He utters the sweet message,
"Come unto Me, all ye that labour and are heavy-laden,
and I will give you rest. Take My yoke upon you, and
learn of Me: for I am meek and lowly in heart: and ye
shall find rest unto your souls. For My yoke is easy, and
My burden is light."[1]

How ready our Jesus was to overcome the evil with the
good. Not only by the dread hours of His passion and
death did He lift off the heavy burden of sin and suffering
from us, but all through His life of self-sacrifice. Every
thought, word, and deed tended to alleviate man's sufferings,
while He ever pointed with words of tender warning to

[1] S. Matt. xi. 28-30.

those spiritual hindrances which cramp the higher life of service and draw souls apart from Him. May we beneath the shadow of our Master's Cross greatly profit by considering together some of those subtle hindrances which beset His saints. Let us not take here wilful rejection, or that host of glaring sins which work openly to destroy souls, but rather those burdens or hindrances which are common to the best and holiest among us. It is a deep subject, full of sad thoughts, shortcomings, omissions, and wanderings. O those multitudinous burdens of a sin-laden world, which no human sympathy can lighten! Do they not point us to a Master Who alone has the power to aid us? Do they not plead with us tenderly to "cast our care upon Him,"[1] for He indeed careth for us? To go to Him, burden-bearers, just as we are, that we may exchange them for His yoke: to learn of Him alone that we may find rest unto our souls.

In Bunyan's Allegory, Christian lost his burden of sin when the Cross of His Master stood out boldly before him. There, alone, can we lose ours—yours and mine—for the cross we bear is too often of our own making. No wonder, then, that it is burdensome. An old writer hath said, " Our cross is too often made of wood grown, nourished, and fostered on our own estate." How can we rise to higher, nobler hopes and aims while thus bowed down with the burdens of selfish indulgence or carnal desires ?

We must learn the better part in the Saviour's School of Self-denial and Suffering, in company with the saints of old. Oh ! those blessed lessons of endurance, patience, abstinence, and sacrifice of self, which the Master gives us from the Cradle to the Grave. Each year we live is a year of grace.

1 1 S. Peter v. 7.

Each Lent we spend with Jesus opens out a new course to
run, and yet it is along the old, old way bearing the footprints
of our Great Cross-bearer, and we must just follow on.   There
is much work to be done—harder lessons to learn—fresh and
more subtle hindrances to meet—more secret sins to overcome ere we can reach the Master's presence.   We can never
have perfect immunity from such hindrances here.   We may,
nay we must, ever pray against them, so that by a continual
warfare we may subdue them, keep them under, as one by
one they arise to hinder our spiritual progress.   We may
root out one or other of them until there are fewer left to
struggle against, or by the aid of the Holy Spirit of Grace,
we may finally wound, weaken or destroy them.   Yet in
some form or other Hindrances will arise to test our
sincerity—to try our strength as disciples until the end, for
the servant so proved shall meet with his due reward if he
persevere courageously in the Master's Cause.

The conflict between good and evil is a real one.   Jesus
requires, nay commands, each to take his side fearlessly,
openly and actively.   There must not be deserters or half-
hearted soldiers in the Master's ranks.   None can be
neutral ; those who do not help, hinder.   " He that
gathereth not with Me, scattereth."[1]   It is a choice of life
and death, and Jesus pleads by His Cross and Passion.
" Come unto Me all ye that are weary and heavy laden, and
I will give you rest."[2]

[1] S. Matt. xii. 30.   [2] S. Matt. xi. 29.

II.

"Take My yoke upon you and learn of Me, and ye shall find rest unto your souls."—S. MATT. XI. 29.

WHAT was the chief characteristic in the Life of Jesus? He came from the eternal presence of the Father of Love to make us by adoption what He is by nature, "Sons of God." He is our Great Leader and Chief. We by nature are followers or disciples. The Great Leaders of this World have not only stamped their names upon the pages of history, whether they have been warriors, statesmen or teachers among men; but they have ruled over nations, made laws and enforced them, and so changed the life and destinies of their subjects. But Jesus, the God-Man, hath done more than this. He hath conquered the human heart; His Kingdom is eternal; His power is unchangeable; His law is Love.

How strange, then, "the whole world lying in wickedness"[1] must have appeared to the All-pure Son of God as He stood alone, misunderstood, tempted, falsely accused, reviled and made to suffer innocently for the sins of men. How those subtle hindrances placed in His way must have pained Him. No wonder He shed tears over the lost city which God had beforetime chosen to set His Name there. Salem, the City of Peace, was to lose that peace and favour with God and man, and henceforth to become illustrious as the scene of the Saviour's Trial, Sufferings and Death. "Behold the Lamb of God, which taketh away the sin of the world."[2] Yes! truly the Victim for thy waywardness and mine. Learn of Him then how to meet thy special hindrances,

---

[1] 1 S. John v. 19.   [2] S. John i. 29.

D

for as the days of our earthly pilgrimage pass on, Satan's
attempts to compass our ruin will wax bolder : the barriers of
evil to keep God out of our lives will be harder to break down.
Do not the lives of the greatest saints prove this? Listen to the
bitter cry of David, " I have sinned and done this evil in
Thy sight," [1] as in deep and true penitence he lamented over
his fall.   Mark the tears of S. Peter, when the tender loving
eyes of his Master searched his very soul, and sent him out
from His presence to weep away the sin. [2] Note the same
truth in S. Paul's confession as he claimed in pure conviction of soul to be the chief among sinners. [3]

So Satan wrestles with us in youth, in middle life, and in
old age : in our hours of strength, and in our moments of
weakness.   " Let him that thinketh he standeth take heed
lest he fall." [4] As we stand with the dark, irrecoverable
past behind us, and the untried, untrodden *future* before us ;
let us use the *present* to the eternal good of our souls by
" Looking unto Jesus, Who *alone* is the Author and Finisher
of our Faith." [5]   Let us turn our eyes inward that we may
know self better ; that we may see ourselves as God sees us
and so be the better able to frame our petitions aright, that
grace may be given to withstand in the evil hour.   May we
daily pray, " Lord, show me Myself," " Lord, show me
Thyself," " Lord, make me like Thee," because a right
view of our faults, or condition, makes of our hindrances
stepping-stones to Heaven.

Among Spiritual hindrances probably *Lukewarmness* stands
out as the most insidious foe inasmuch as it confronts all.
It is at all times a special danger to religious persons.   It
proclaims that we have done well in the past ; that we have

[1] Ps. li. 4.   [2] S. Matt. xxvi. 75.   [3] 1 Tim. i. 15.
            [4] 1 Cor. x. 12.   [5] Heb. xii. 2.

climbed Heaven's ladder a certain height, and then from
sheer weariness or cold indifference, we have given up. We
must ever remember that he who has never been religious
can never be lukewarm.

When this special temptation assails us let us betake
ourselves to prayer. Here alone is the only antidote against
the evil which poisons the soul! To persevere in prayer!
If we become lukewarm what will be our condition? How
will God and the Angels see us? We may go to Church
and take part outwardly in the Services as others do; yet
there will be no reality—no zeal—no fervour—no offering
from the heart of Praise, Prayer and Thanksgiving—No
confession of evils done—No depth in our Worship—No
seeking after God. We may read our Bible simply as an
old habit, or duty, without loving it, or finding its spiritual
message to our souls, and yet those Sacred Books are letters
of love and warning from our God in Heaven.

We may go to the Blessed Sacrament but not hungrily,
without any desire to be refreshed and strengthened at the
Lord's Table. There will be no longing after holiness—no
spiritual feeding where lukewarmness sets in. Again, in
our Private Prayers and Meditations there will be but little
devotion; zeal will fade; faith and hope will droop their
heads like flowers needing the refreshing raindrop or dew
of God's presence and power. There, the very inner life
of the soul is stricken as with a deadly disease, for the
lukewarm are much afraid of the world's opinion. They
are careful not to grow over-religious. They will have no
Elijahs with severe, ascetic rules of life; no John the
Baptists with pointed warnings against sin. No! all must
go on smoothly and pleasantly in the world's groove, while
Satan craftily whispers false peace, "Just this once," "Do

as others do." So drop by drop the poison of sloth, selfish ease and indifference chills the soul and steels the heart against the warmth of a Saviour's loving invitation, "Come unto Me, and I will refresh you, and ye shall find rest unto your souls."[1]

Oh, lukewarm Christians, take the Master's yoke and learn of Him. Once you were Baptized—given to God—filled with the Holy Ghost: Once you were Confirmed—made strong—endued with power from on high: Once you made your First Communion in penitence and lively faith: Where are those promises and zeal of other days? There was no lukewarmness then. Then, the heart as a garden filled with sweet flowers spread abroad its fragrance to God, Who gazed upon it with joy as the Divine Gardener, His Holy Spirit of Love, tended and trained the fragile stems and opening buds, while Heaven's dews freshened and quickened it. Now, those flowers are drooping—the petals are limp—the beauty is well-nigh faded—the dying light of Love is flickering within thee—thy Guardian Angel is weeping o'er thee while Satan stands triumphant beside thee in thine hour of extreme peril. Lift up the bowed head and raise thine eyes to Jesus dying, and say "*For me*" ere it be too late.

O! Holy Saviour, Refresh, Renew, these hearts of ours!

[1] S. Matt. xi. 29.

III.

" Take My yoke upon you and learn of Me . . . . and ye shall find rest unto your souls."—S. MATT. XI. 29.

WHAT a subtle evil is Lukewarmness! Its gentle and well-nigh unconscious growth makes it the more to be feared and dreaded. It creeps upon us unawares. One by one of the human powers and faculties it weans from God's service, until enthroned in the heart it defies His Almighty Power, and asserted by man's Free Will ignores His Holy Presence. No wonder then that God hates lukewarmness. No wonder then that the Church bids us pray against it; that our Heavenly Father may show " to them that be in error the light of His Truth, to the intent that they may *return* into the way of righteousness."[1]

" Well may I guess and feel why Autumn should be sad ;
  But vernal airs should sorrow heal, Spring should be gay and glad ;
  Yet as along the violet bank I rove, the languid sweetness seems to
    choke my breath,
  I set me down beside the hazel grove,
  And sigh, and half could wish my weariness were death."[2]

Then lukewarmness is such a dishonour to God—to our Jesus and Saviour. He Who gave Himself for us, asks, Is there so little to attract in Him ? We desire to be a Hero in the world : Where is our zeal for God's Service ? We cling to earthly friends in love : Why are the arms not stretched out to Jesus ? Lukewarmness provokes God to punish us ; Lukewarmness ruins souls, for it is the influence of Satan to blight and wither the spiritual life implanted by God.

[1] Coll. III. Sun. after Easter.   [2] Keble's "Christian Year," III. Sun. after Trinity.

There will be a time when we shall yearn for zeal misplaced, when the hot tears of remorse will tell of faith deadened and hope deferred, for the once pure, bright sinless life of child-hood will appeal to us after years of neglect and indifference. It may be on the bed of death when human ties are being severed, and earthly things are passing from us—when all other language is forgotten, that the old childhood's Prayers and Hymns well up in our memory, those sweet, old Prayers and Hymns once lisped out in innocence and faith at Mother's knee. What sweet memories of the past !

We all know about our spiritual failings ; we are fully aware of our pet habits of sin, and yet we just lack the zeal and courage to cast them out. We all need arousing from this indifference and self-satisfaction ; we all need to be awakened from the drowsiness of sin. Lent is a season of spiritual reparation ; Jesus the Divine Sufferer pleads with us by His noble example, to leave the world and its allurements that we may be with Him : to cast away the old habits—the burden which is so pleasant, and yet so grievous that we may take His yoke of self-sacrifice. Let us turn our eyes and hearts from the world and its vanities that we may look Heaven-ward. How truly sad is a life of habitual sin ! Is it not a living death ? Living without God—without Jesus, Who declared Himself to be the Resurrection and the Life, each day we drift silently—almost unconsciously along the flood of sin away from God.

This brings us to another deadly barrier, another subtle hindrance, that keeps God out of our daily lives. I mean " *Luxury, or Spiritual Sloth.*" It is near of kin to Luke-warmness, and yet it is more for it exists by the gratifica-tion of the carnal desires, and places the interests and care of the body above the care of the spiritual, so the soul falls into neglect. The great antidote for *Self-indulgence* is its opposite virtue, *Self-denial*. Here again we must enter the school of Jesus and learn of Him to overcome evil with good. We must endeavour to live more by rule. A regulated life is a blessed thing because it just keeps bodily comfort from becoming softness to us. A life which just keeps a check upon us must remind us that we are Disciples of a Higher Master ; Cross-bearers and fellow-sufferers with Him. O Blessed Jesus make us to realize the full beauty and dignity of such a title !

Too many of us are simply content with leading a regular life. This is simply keeping fairly straight. It may be abstaining from excess in living or pleasure, yet still leading a negative sort of life—aimless—useless—because doing little harm, yet little good. Not doing actual wrong, yet leaving the right undone. In such a life there can be no contrition, because there exists no discomfort from sin : there can be no confession of sin for the heart is deceived, and the mind is deadened. The false peace and security are gained by a comparison of Pharisaical goodness of self with the glaring evils seen in others living around us. Is not this a truly dangerous state ? How may we guard against it ? Learn of Jesus to overcome all that hinders—that mars God's image in us. Be more guarded in thought, word and deed. Be not lukewarm or slothful in spiritual things. A saint of God but lately passed from us hath said, "Christ's life will shew what the evil is. Christ's death hath atoned for it. Let us repent and live—the Character of Jesus is our Model. To study Him is our simple duty. One by one His features must be studied—must be copied, if we would gain His likeness and approval. There is no safety—no peace, still less perfection short of this. Learn thy lesson well, O loving disciple."[1]

1 " The Worship of Heaven," by Rev. D. Trinder, M.A.

IV.

"Lead us not into temptation, but deliver us from evil."

—S. MATT. VI. 13.

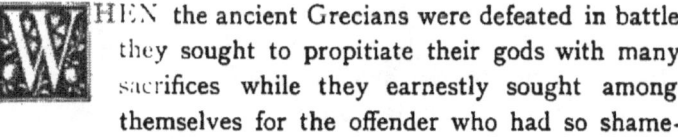

HEN the ancient Grecians were defeated in battle they sought to propitiate their gods with many sacrifices while they earnestly sought among themselves for the offender who had so shame-lessly brought this evil upon their nation. So the true disciple when he falls in the spiritual race should seek for the weakness—should search out the cause of stumbling and offence, that he may rise to fall no more by the same evil.

Satan is ever ready to devise new methods—more attractive plans, to encompass our spiritual downfall, therefore we have much need of daily prayer for strength during temptation—for sure deliverance from evil. Another spiritual web of Satan's is *Prejudice in holy things*. So common has this hin-drance become that men too often, alas, stand up as champions for God under its shadow and protection. Nay, even the very weapons they use to attack souls bear this same title, so subtle and misleading is it to them. Prejudice proves a state of bondage as a spiritual hindrance. It implies that we have drawn a circle, narrow and full of conceit it may be in its boundary, and yet we delude ourselves that it shall contain all that is precious and worth possessing in the Life and Understanding. In our ignorance we close the eye of Faith, while we declare, " It is enough I cannot see beyond. God is only to be found in this place." It may need a voice from Heaven to turn us from our purpose, even as Saul heard, saying, " I am Jesus, Whom thou

persecutest : it is hard for thee to kick against the pricks."[1]
For prejudice is not a virtue implanted by the Holy Spirit
of Grace ; it is rather an opposing of self-will and human
knowledge, frail and weak though it be, to God's Divine
Will and Unchangeable Laws.

It is a solemn thing to find men choosing their own religion
in the same spirit as they select their clothing, or other
earthly possessions, to suit their own tastes, without giving
one thought to the question, *What is Religion ?* Yet it hath
been declared that " Religion is a rule that we follow to
regulate our lives here, and the standard by which hereafter
we may be judged." Thus if we choose our religion to wear
only as a garment it will soon become shabby and threadbare.

Religion cannot be put on and cast off at the will or
caprice of man. It must proceed from the heart, and so
illuminate the whole life as the Spirit of Light directs from
within. Jesus taught, " some fell upon a rock."[2] Yes, there
may still be shallow Christians who in time of trial fall
away ; yet One died to teach thee the better way of Life.
Learn then, O erring disciple, that Prejudice is a polite
denial of God's love—a setting aside of Christ's salvation—
a taking to ourselves of other guides than the Holy Spirit
of Grace. Surely we need to cry earnestly for deliverance
from this evil—to pray that we may still cling to the guiding
Hand of God in this time of trial. Our safety then lies in
prayer for meekness, for a teachable heart, for more faith, a
firmer hope. " From all blindness of heart ; from all false
doctrine, heresy and schism ; Good Lord, deliver us."[3] Let
us pray on until light comes for believe me there is a mystery
in our poor prayers hidden away. " A Value in them which
flows from the fact that God Himself in Jesus—our Jesus—

---

[1] Acts ix. 5.   [2] S. Luke viii. 6.   [3] Litany.

the perfect Man, knelt on the cold slopes of Olivet to pour out His pure soul in prayer."[1]   Even so.   He will deliver us. " He will not suffer us to be tempted above that we are able, but with the temptation will make a way of escape, lest we fall into Satan's power."[2]

Again let us beware of *Self-pride*.   Spiritual ambition is a dangerous feeling which exalts us before self only to hurl us headlong down the narrow path of humility and holy fear which leads to God.

If we trust in self alone like the Pharisee in the Parable, and so far forget our need of grace and mercy, we shall go " *Unhelped* " away from God.   A wise saying of olden days bade men to " Always look up to God rather than down on others."   S. Paul, the faithful champion of his Master's cause, hath declared for our example, " Christ died to save sinners of whom I am chief."[3]   It is a dangerous state to become blinded by our own righteousness for then we see not temptation ere it approaches to ensnare us—we exalt ourselves by parading our religion rather than living it, yet the Master teaches, " Blessed are the poor in spirit : for theirs is the Kingdom of Heaven."[4]

If we must be kings, let us remember that the grandest dominion is to rule " *Self*."   Why this feverish ambition to be above—better than our fellows ?   Jesus, thy Master and mine, reigned from the Tree of Shame.   His crown was of thorns, He wore a suffering diadem for thee and me.   Yet religious people envy one another—brood over supposed wrongs— become dissatisfied with their spiritual lot.   Oh ! compare thy condition with thy Master's, and learn of Him that " ye may find rest unto your souls."[5]

[1] Rev. F. La Trobe Bateman, M.A.   [2] 1 Cor. x. 13.   [3] 1 Tim. i. 15.
[4] S. Matt. v. 3.   [5] S. Matt. xi. 29.

The lily of the valley in its snow-white purity hides its beauty in the deepest shade. The lowly violet, sweetest among flowers in fragrance, bends its head earthwards, and must be sought after to be found. The chief of songsters pours out its canticle of praise in the still hours of night, and the lark of heaven seeks the ground whereon to build its nest and rear its young. So learn from God's Book of Nature, even from birds and flowers to bend thy proud neck beneath the Master's yoke.

V.

"Lead us not into temptation; but deliver us from evil."
—S. MATT. VI. 13.

THERE is a critical moment when we find ourselves alone with the Tempter. God is forgotten, and trusting to our own strength we are soon overcome; or the knowledge that God is with us, and He Who alone knows our true strength—what we are able to bear, gives us power to cast down our enemy. It is a struggle for Victory. Yet Temptation gives a new claim to God's faithfulness if used aright, for the fiery trials alone can bring out the true strength of character. What is thy special besetting sin? Where is the weakness in thy spiritual stronghold, O Christian? What is the loose stone which Satan so warily places to cause thee to stumble over? What is that rank weed which creeps so insidiously between the stones of thy spiritual fabric to loosen its joints? Is it envy? or uncharitableness?—A measuring of thy own spiritual stature by the shortcomings of others? If so, take thy burden—thy trouble to the great Burden-bearer as He stretches forth His Sacred Arms to draw thee unto Himself for He hath put away thy sin in His one perfected Sacrifice, Oblation and Satisfaction before God on Calvary's Throne.

Yes, there is work to do for thee and me as disciples. We must expect temptations. " Be sober, be. vigilant; because your adversary the devil, as a roaring lion, walketh about, seeking whom he may devour. Whom resist stedfast in the faith, knowing that the same afflictions are accomplished in your brethren that are in the world."[1]

To win the Crown of Righteousness we must first bear the Cross of Suffering with Jesus. Therefore we must ever be watchful—we must make constant preparation. " Watch and pray that ye enter not into temptation : the spirit indeed is willing, but the flesh is weak,"[2] said the Holy Jesus, when in the Garden of Gethsemane He found His disciples sleeping instead of watching with Him in His hour of agony and prayer. " Temptation has been compared to the golden apple thrown into the path of duty. We meet with it in the wilderness, on the mountain top, even on the pinnacle of the Temple; in the School of Christ, where Judas fell ; in Paradise, where Eve became the handmaid of Satan ; in Heaven itself, whence the Devil was cast out."[3]

> "Christian seek not yet repose,
>   Hear Thy Guardian Angel say ;
>   Thou art in the midst of foes ;
>   Watch and pray."[4]

We have already seen that the Devil suits his Temptations to our tastes. He studies carefully our likes and

[1] r S. Peter v. 8, 9.   [2] S. Matt. xxvi. 41.
[3] Rev. xii. 9.   " Notes on Catechisings," by a London Vicar.
[4] Hymns A. & M., 269.

dislikes until he ensnares us in the meshes of sin. The golden bowl of temptation too often contains the deadly draught, so God in His infinite mercy holds us back from it. Jesus in the Wilderness and on the Cross hath vanquished our common foe, and the Holy Spirit of Grace abideth still within us to strengthen us in the hour of need.

Will not this explain God's mysterious dealings with us His beloved children ? Sometimes " Wealth " goes, lest we should grow covetous and worldly. Then again " Influence " wanes to keep us from growing self-righteous. The " health of the body " departs, lest we be led to place it before the immortal soul.

In our ignorance and blindness we cry, This is indeed hard ! Yes, disciple, it is the hard immovable Rock of thy Saviour's Love. " The same yesterday, to-day, and for ever."[1] To win thee, O wanderer, back to Himself. " Commit thy way unto the Lord and put thy trust in Him ; and He shall bring it to pass."[2]

" Lead us not into temptation, but deliver us from evil," for Thou knowest our infirmities, and the power and utmost malice of our enemies.

Thou knowest how to deliver the godly out of temptation.[3] Grant, O God, that we may never run into those temptations which in our prayers we desire to avoid.

" Vouchsafe to us the gift of perseverance on which our eternal happiness depends.

" Lord, never permit our trials to be above our strength. O Holy Spirit of grace, be not wanting to us in the hour of temptation. And in all temptations give us power to resist and overcome them. Leave us not in the power of

[1] Heb. xiii. 8.   [2] Ps. xxxvii. 5.   [3] 2 S. Peter ii. 9.

evil spirits to ruin us.   Support us under all our saving
trials and troubles."[1]

"O most powerful Advocate! I put my cause into Thy
Hands; Let it be unto Thy servant according to this word;
let Thy Blood and merits plead for my pardon; say unto
me, as Thou didst unto the penitent in Thy Gospel, 'Thy
sins are forgiven.'   And grant that I may live to bring
forth fruits meet for repentance."[2]

For the life *offered to Thee in Holy Baptism*, will be *preserved
and guided by Thee on earth*, and *received by Thee in glory. Amen.*

THE LIFE OF FORGIVENESS.

I.

" Let all bitterness, and wrath, and anger, and clamour, and evil-
speaking, be put away from you, with all malice : And be ye kind one
to another, tender-hearted, forgiving one another, even as God for
Christ's sake hath forgiven you."—EPHES. IV. 31, 32.

HAT a truly marvellous appeal to the lives and
souls of his brethren at Ephesus, the Apostle Paul
makes in these words!   What a finished picture
drawn from that most perfect life of his Divine
Master, is presented to us here.   The greatest of the great
Theological virtues is here sketched in simple, tender
language to win us back from evil.   One by one, the old
familiar sins are enumerated in all their subtle power and
deadliness, that the soul-healing antidote may the more
effectually appeal to our higher natures as scholars in the
School of Jesus, Who is the keynote to the whole passage.

How vividly do we see that Sacred Life of Suffering

---

[1] Bp. Wilson's "Sacra Privata."   [2] Idem.

portrayed under those dark words, "bitterness, wrath, anger, clamour, evil-speaking, malice," with which the sin-darkened world heralded His presence, and brought about His Death ! How gently, yet how fully, also falls the Divine Light of that Life of self-sacrifice, shedding pardon, love, kindness, tenderness and mercy upon all.

"For this our Jesus died : for this He lives."

And we too would learn the higher Lesson of Divine Love.

In that old familiar prayer we have lisped out from childhood's happy days, we find those two wonderful words, "Give" and "Forgive." Both in their depth and sim-plicity belong to God, " Who givest all : "[1] Yet we as His true and faithful children have to take them into our hearts and lives, and so prove to others that we are indeed worthy of the Name we bear. Can we do this ?

We acknowledge that we need daily pardon as we need daily bread. There are those duties owing to God and man still unpaid. Wrongs, debts, omissions, wanderings, marked against us daily, need Forgiveness. Each day brings new debts, and so we must not leave the old ones unpaid. God each day invites us to go to Him for mercy, yet only if we really feel the need of it. This is the true life-germ of all penitence. It was so in the old story of the Prodigal's return. "When he came to himself he said, How many hired servants of my father's have bread enough and to spare, and I perish with hunger !"[2] Here the true need asserted itself. It is only when we realise the value of Mercy—Pardon full and free, can we rightly shew it to others. A Saint of other days hath said, " The unforgiving

[1] Acts xvii. 25.   [2] S. Luke xv. 17.

man dare not say to God the words he acts to others, 'Forgive me not.'"

It is often a help to us to regard spiritual matters in the light of secular ones. Too often, alas! we know how the wayward and erring child gives anxiety, sorrow, and aching hearts to its parents. Oh! consider what a pang goes to the heart of God our Father as day by day we rebel and reject His love! The words, "Forgive us, as we forgive them," contain a just motto, loudly demanded from us by the world—"Do as you would be done by." Yet human forgiveness must ever fall far short of Divine forgiveness. The hundred pence can never be compared to the ten thousand talents. Yet the principle remains the same. All acknowledge the truth and justice of these words, while so few of us are able to act up to them.

II.

"Forgive us our debts, as we forgive our debtors."—S. MATT. VI. 12.

F all the Saviour's commands, "Love one another,"[1] and "Forgive as ye would be forgiven,"[2] are undoubtedly the most difficult to carry out. At the outset the human heart rebels, and in our selfish worldliness we say, "Impossible! It can't be done. Bid me regard—esteem—venerate—look up to—or even like all men, and I will try to do my best; but to love them is quite another thing."

And why is this so? Simply because Love springs from within—Love is called forth by some hidden power—Love conquers all things—"Love than Death itself more strong"

[1] S. John xv. 12. [2] S. Luke vi. 37.

can never take the second place—may not be commanded,
or bidden to act at the will of others. And so with Forgiveness. We may forget an insult, or live down a grievance.
We may gloss over an offence, or pass by an affront, but
command me to "Forgive!" Never! My very spirit
rebels against the thought. Forgiveness is so hard, and
yet so necessary. And yet—

> "Far better than all forgetting
> Is the wonderful word, 'Forgive.'"

Let us try to think it all out.

What is Forgiveness? It is not merely suspension of
punishment, or a calm and passive assent to wrong-doing
called "overlooking this once." It is not even a restoring
of the lost friendship, as shown forth by the warm grasp of
the hand, or the pleasant, though silent language of the
eyes—It is far more than this!

To learn Forgiveness we must alone feel it. It is a
special grace implanted by God, and called forth by the
hidden power within us. Ask the little child weeping away
its first sin under the gentle influence of a mother's pardon—
Ask the criminal reprieved as he stands before the bar of
judgment—Ask the once wayward, yet now repentant,
Prodigal returned to his Father's breast—What is Forgiveness? Such as these alone understand its power. What
words then may describe the sweetness, depth, comfort and
peace of Forgiveness?

Let us deny not to others then what is so precious to ourselves. Again, Forgiveness belongs to God rather than to
man, for [1] "God our Father is never swayed by passion; . . .
With Him the All-merciful and Just One there is no vindic-

[1] Rev. Brooke Lambert's "Sermons on the Lord's Prayer."

E

tiveness which is gratified by inflicting pain—there is no sense of injury seeking relief against the wrong doer." God simply punishes to put away evil—to destroy sin. He the All-pure must destroy all that is impure and unholy.

Here then may we find our starting point—"*With God.*" From Him alone we must learn our first lesson in Forgiveness.

" God loves Me." " I have sinned against God." " God wants me back again."

So one poor Penitent came to himself and realised that sin—his pet habits—his daily thoughts, words, acts of evil, wanderings, had separated—alienated him from his God. Therefore God's punishment is Love. I know that it is difficult to grasp this. Here again surely we may learn from the earthly picture.

" We find the word Forgiveness changes as Life goes on. Forgive me, pleads the child, and I will never do it again. Here the cry for pardon is prompted from the lowest motive—to escape punishment ; but as the child grows the motive changes."[1] There may be no particular dread of pain, yet the disgrace which follows the evil done calls forth fear. To be called a coward is then far worse than physical suffering. Now Forgiveness means a restoring to confidence—A Blotting out the old score—A Forgetting or putting away of the penalty due to wrong doing. Then arises from within a motive still higher—purer—nobler than these. Duty bids us view Right and Wrong in the true light, and so we learn to undo the Wrong—unlive the evil done—and dare to do the Right as a manly duty.

Thus while we cry for Pardon for the past, we are led to extend the Heart of Love, and the Hand of Forgiveness, to

[1] Rev. Brooke Lambert's " Sermons on the Lord's Prayer."

others in the present. The thought that God loves me—trusts me—is ever ready to forgive me—keeps me from wrong doing far more than any fear of punishment or shame of disgrace can.

III.

"If ye do not forgive, neither will your Father which is in Heaven forgive you your trespasses."—S. MARK XI. 26.

HEN we cry for Forgiveness then, we ask for deliverance from the penalty deserved—we cry for pardon for evil done—and we plead for power to forgive our brethren also.

The Church in Her Services teaches us to say " We—Us—Our," and in the General Confession after acknow-ledging and confessing our manifold sins and wickedness, we plead in deep contrition that all, even our enemies, may be spared from punishment and restored to favour by our Father in Heaven. Do we mean it ? If not, we cannot really be in earnest about our own pardon. Too many of us need David's "*clean heart*" and "*right spirit*." We lack zeal in our penitence—we need more earnestness in placing our dark catalogue of sins committed before God at the mercy-seat of Heaven.

How many scenes of pardon crowd around the Saviour's life and mission ! Those sweetly pathetic stories of " The Lost Sheep," " The Lost Coin," and " The Prodigal Son," teach us the deeper mysteries of pardoning love. " Even as God for Christ's sake hath forgiven you."[1]

[1] Ephes. iv. 22.

" ' Lord, Thou hast here Thy Ninety and Nine, Are they not enough
  for Thee ? '
But the Shepherd made answer, ' This of Mine hath wandered away
  from Me ;
And through the desert and over the steep I must wander on till I
  find My Sheep.' "

That wanderer was thy soul and mine.

What it cost the Shepherd to bring us back, only Calvary's
story can tell. Once again : How much the Heart of God
is revealed in Forgiveness ? Why do we pray, *Forgive us ?*
Because our sins do not end with ourselves, any more
than a terrible disease remains in one spot. One of the
most awful revelations of the future may be—" The evil
we have done to others." May we in our day of mercy
take this to heart, and pray sincerely, earnestly, faithfully,
" As we forgive them that trespass against us, O Lord."
We must ever remember that their sin may have been caused
by our own shortcomings : they may have first caught the
infection from us. How can we then refuse to pardon for
petty wrong done ; for cruel mistake, or unintentional insult
offered. How can we hug our grievances, or cherish our
ill-feelings, while we remember that Jesus has declared that
there is no limit to Forgiveness, and the Father of Love
awaits our return to Him to tell all the sad tale of wrong
done and duties left undone, as we lay our wearying burden
before Him for pardon full and free.

How truly sad to think that I am still unable to forgive
that brother—that sister—for whom Christ died—that I
cannot yet pray the words, " Spare, and restore them, O
Father." Yes, surely there must be something wrong here.

Learn, O erring disciple, in mercy to forgive that thou
mayest be forgiven.

Think it all out. What is thy injury, thy loss, or thy wrong, compared with thy God's ? Look to Calvary— " Even as God for Christ's sake hath forgiven you."[1] Read there inscribed, " FOR ME," with tear-stained eyes of penitence.

That Cross of Shame and Suffering was raised FOR THEE AND ME. Hearken to that sweet cry for mercy ever proceeding from the lips of our dear Saviour and Mediator— " FATHER, forgive them, for they know not what they do,"[2] and so mayest thou learn Forgiveness in the School of Jesus that thine own pardon may be sealed before the Throne of God. *Amen.*

> " Just as I am, Thou wilt receive,
> Wilt welcome, pardon, cleanse, relieve:
> Because Thy promise I believe,
> O Lamb of God, I come, I come."[3]

[1] Eph. iv. 32.   [2] S. Luke xxiii. 34.   [3] Hymns A. & M., 255, verse 4.

" THERE ARE THESE THREE ELEMENTS IN THE CUP AND BAPTISM OF
JESUS WHICH GIVES IT ITS SUPREME AND EXEMPLARY VALUE—LONELI-
NESS, AND MARTYRDOM, AND SACRIFICE."
    —" *Questions of Faith and Duty,*" *by Bishop Thorold of Winchester.*

" SINCE BLOOD IS FITTEST, LORD, TO WRITE
    THY SORROWS IN, AND BLOODY FIGHT ;
    MY HEART HATH STORE ; WRITE THEN : WHERE, IN
    ONE BOX, DOTH LIE BOTH INK AND SIN.

THAT WHEN SIN SPIES SO MANY FOES,
    THY WHIPS, THY NAILS, THY WOUNDS, THY WOES,
    ALL COME TO LODGE THERE, SIN MAY SAY,
    'NO ROOM FOR ME,' AND FLY AWAY.

SIN BEING GONE, OH ! FILL THE PLACE,
    AND KEEP POSSESSION—WITH THY GRACE ;
    LEST SIN TAKE COURAGE, AND RETURN,
    AND ALL THE WRITINGS BLOT OR BURN."
                —*From George Herbert's " Good Friday."*

The Preaching of the Cross.

PART II.

LEARN OF JESUS

HOW TO DIE!

"HATH HE NOT ALWAYS TREASURES, ALWAYS FRIENDS,
  THE GOOD, GREAT MAN?—THREE TREASURES, LOVE AND LIGHT,
AND CALM THOUGHT, REGULAR AS INFANTS' BREATH ;
  AND THREE FIRM FRIENDS, MORE SURE THAN DAY AND NIGHT—
HIMSELF, HIS MAKER, AND THE ANGEL DEATH."
                                        —*Coleridge.*

"I HAVE FOUND HIM WHOM MY SOUL LOVETH."—*Cant. iii. 4.*

DEATH.

I.

" And it was the third hour, and they Crucified Him."—S. MARK XV. 25.

IT is surely a solemn duty which has called us from the world at this holy season. We are appointed watchers—witnesses of a remarkable scene—a death-bed—even the rough, cruel bed of sorrows of our Divine Master—Jesus.

> " Who died that we might be forgiven ;
> Who died to make us good ;
> That we might go at last to Heaven,
> Saved by His precious Blood."

We would meditate together upon the scenes of the first Good Friday, the death-day of our dear Lord, and Love—earnest Love, hath drawn us from the office, the workshop, or the varied occupations of life, to watch—" to mourn with Him awhile," at the foot of His Cross. Good Friday comes laden with many thoughts, yet Death by reason of its true Impressiveness, and great Solemnity, seems to take the foremost place : yet behind the shadowy figure Death there looms one far more dreadful, more to be feared, and hated, for it bears upon its breast the one word, " Sin." It points to the mysterious past, where Man made in the image of his Creator, possessing an immortal soul implanted by God, having lost his dignity and " the beauty of holiness," stands disgraced, ashamed, and filled with fear. With downcast eyes, and bowed head, he is driven out of the Paradise planted for his special existence by God's love. It is but two fallen souls who shrink from the clear, bright gaze of the angel guard at the gates, yet how much follows, and depends upon that outward journey from Paradise, only Calvary's story can tell. The tiny rill of sin soon became a swollen river rushing ever onward away from God until the roar of an angry flood greeted the Sinless Sufferer—Jesus ; and we stand dismayed with awe and wonder to see the issue in the story of the First Good Friday. Go apart then to " Behold the Lamb of God which taketh away the sin of the World." [1] Hear His gentle voice still asking individual souls, " Lovest thou Me ? " [2]—" Behold and see if there be any sorrow like unto My sorrow ? " [3]

What must this world have appeared like to the pure and holy Jesus ? On every side greeted Him the existence or traces of sin. Sorrow—sickness—want—misery—strife—pride—and disobedience He saw plainly stamped upon the bodies and souls of sin-laden men and women. How much it must have cost His great Heart of love and mercy to have left His Father's Home on high to seek and to save these unhappy lost ones ! What an incongruous multitude of suffering !—What chaos and confusion !—What a terrible army of dreaded foes met the Great Master's gaze as with compassion He beheld the thoughts and deeds of men during His quiet suffering life of mercy, or when watching them in His death agony from His Cross of shame.

May not the voice of the disciple enquire, " O my Jesus, how cruel is the death Thou sufferest ! Vouchsafe, then, to tell me, what led Thee to submit to this cruel death ? " When the answer cometh sweetly, " My love for thee, it

---

[1] S. John i. 29.   [2] S. John xxi. 15.   [3] Lam. i. 12.

was, that has nailed Me to this Cross."[1] This then is the solemn secret of that wonderful scene, which destroyed and gained a final victory over Sin and Death—even Infinite, Ineffable Love—Love deeper, stronger, than the love of a mother. Even God's love as revealed in Jesus—the Redeemer of men's souls.

II.

"For since by man came death, by man came also the resurrection of the dead."—I COR. XV. 21.

WHAT is Death? This dread messenger who comes to all? Death is both the end and the beginning. It is a laying aside of the earthly garments toil stained and well worn, for the putting on of the Robe of Eternal Life. It is our Jordan which divides us from the promised Land—"Heaven." Weary pilgrims still hasten to its banks to lay down their burdens, yet they shrink from it as the cold Valley draws nearer. The new Life lies beyond. The Master's feet have crossed the Flood, and He waits but on the other side for us. "Rejoice," He calls, "To-day shalt thou be with Me in Paradise."[2] And then the veil drops, and we cannot pierce beyond into the joys and mysteries of the Great Unseen, for the Prophet declareth, "Who knoweth the spirit of man that goeth upwards."[3]

Death, the severance of human ties and friendships brings sadness, and rightly so, because rebellion of will disorganised human nature. Therefore where sin is there

[1] Meditation on "The Suffering Life on Earth." Translated by Bp. Forbes.
[2] S. Luke xxiii. 43.   [3] Eccles. iii. 21.

is Death, and the Crowning Example hangs on Calvary's Cross for the sin not His own.

"Thus the Passion of Jesus has ever been the source of wonder and contemplation to the people of God. In it the marvels of Divine Love towards men are, as it were, summed up, and presented to our eyes in one stupendous act of mercy and deliverance. As we gaze upon the uplifted figure of the Crucified, hanging between Heaven and earth, pierced with bleeding wounds by members of that race, whose form and nature He has for ever conjoined with His Godhead : As we behold Him, made a spectacle to men and angels, dying between two common malefactors, we seem to see inscribed beneath the Tree of Shame, ' So God loved the world.' "[1] *So God loves my soul.*

This then is our Good Friday Lesson. Glad tidings of Love—Love declared by suffering—" Hereby perceive we the love of God, because He laid down His life for us."[3] And again, " We love—because He first loved us."[4] That which came forth from the pure bosom of God cannot but lead us to return thither as children of His love—so Love begets love.

What comfort, hope and light is shed abroad from the death scene of Jesus to guide us onward and upward nearer to Him.—It is a ladder of hope to every weary Jacob in this wilderness of sin.—It is the way to Heaven, even the way of the Cross. The disciple is not above his Master. " It is enough for the disciple that he be as his Master."[5] So we must take up the Cross at the Master's bidding, and count it both gain and glory to bear it in His Name and for His Service. Suffering has been sanctified in Jesus, and

[1] Rev. W. Skeffington, " The Sinless Sufferer," I., pp. 1, 2.   [3] S. John iii. 16.
[3] 1 S. John iii. 16.   [4] 1 S. John iv. 19.   [5] S. Matt. x. 25.

His Love supports all. May this be the spirit of our meditations. May we lose self, and find Jesus. May we, guided by the Holy Spirit of Grace, learn the true nature of Sin, and flee to Jesus, the Conqueror—the Life-Giver—Who alone declares, " I am the Resurrection and the Life."[1] Let the Cross of Jesus tell its own sweet story of suffering, pardon and love to our weary, sin-laden souls. Yes! that poor, deserted, insulted Sufferer was " The Son of God." Our salvation depends on this truth. Who did it? The Jews! Yes! but you and I also had a share in it. The thorns which sprang from the first sin pierced the Sacred Brow of the Second Adam—Your Jesus and Mine. Our sins were nailed in those Hands of Benediction. Behold! how God hates sin!—How God loves the sinner! Let us use this Holy Season for meditation in sweet communion with our Jesus while He pours out the very secrets of His great Heart of Love. Let us ask prayerfully the Holy Spirit to keep our poor wandering hearts from fluttering to earthly things. Let each effort be an adoration to our suffering King!—each silent prayer a true offering of the secrets of our hearts and lives. Let us pour out to our Dying Friend and Brother, all we feel for Him—for others—for self.

"O Jesus, Captain of our great salvation,
    Help us to follow in Thy footsteps, Lord;
And both in gladness, and in dread temptation,
    Still to be true to Thee, and keep Thy Word." *Amen.*

[1] S. John xi. 25.

THE GREAT INTERCESSOR.

I.

FIRST WORD.

" Father, forgive them, for they know not what they do."
— S. LUKE XXIII. 34.

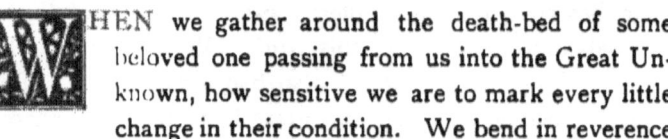HEN we gather around the death-bed of some beloved one passing from us into the Great Unknown, how sensitive we are to mark every little change in their condition. We bend in reverence to catch their last words, so that we may prove our love by carrying out their requests, and we treasure up every look or movement for solemn, calm reflection in the future. Yes, the secrets of life are often disclosed then—breathed out from the dying pillow. Some, revealing moments and acts of horrible sin in the piteous cry for pardon uttered ; others, calmly resigning the life lived in faith, hope, and love, into their Father's keeping.

Good Friday's Passion scene reveals three remarkable death-beds. Jesus in the midst hanging between the two malefactors, the one *penitent*, the other *hardened* by the sufferings of those last hours. Each sufferer revealed the secrets of his soul : so that in the last words of the Sinless Sufferer we read His very Self—the nearest and dearest wishes of that Noble Heart appear in those Seven Words of Love which fell from the Saviour's lips. Should not we treasure them as the legacy bequeathed to us by our best Friend ? Truly the Passion of Jesus, began, continued, and ended in Prayer. His first cry revealed to us His true Nature. It was a loving cry for mercy, pardon full and free for His enemies, who yet clamoured for His death—who mocked His patient sufferings—who scorned His gentle submission to their cruel acts, not knowing that it was for their salvation He was content to die this shameful death. And now, O sinner, "Behold your King !"[1]—Nay rather, "Behold your God!" The way of sorrows has been trodden, Calvary is reached at last. That suffering, deserted One hath borne His heavy Cross for thee and me. A dread weight because pressed down by the full catalogue of human sin and misery. No wonder the Divine Sufferer fell exhausted beneath His load. Yet He shrinks not from paying the full penalty. " Thy Will be done "[2] seems to strengthen His pale and trembling body, as He willingly allows His murderers to pass the nails through those tender Hands and Feet. Yet was this Innocent Sufferer silent ! He uttered no complaint. He kept His eyes fixed on Heaven, and offered to God for our salvation His sufferings and His life. O brothers, what a silent reproof to our wayward wills. The Saviour teaches us truly how to live—how to die ! All my impatience, murmuring, self-will and selfishness cries for pardon as I behold His silent agony. "Thy Will be done,"[3] has a deeper meaning for me now, when I see that the world which Satan had gained through sin can only be won back to God by the Cross. Why do I love Him so little, and serve Him so ill ? Why am I so slothful, lukewarm, when Thou, O my Jesus, art so in earnest as to die for me ?

"Jesus, my Lord, I Thee adore—O make me love Thee more and more."

[1] S. John vi. 14.　　　[2] S. Matt. vi. 10.　　　[3] S. Matt. vi. 10.

II.

" Pray for them which despitefully use you, and persecute you."
—S. MATT. V. 44.

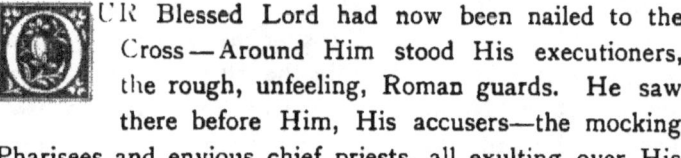UR Blessed Lord had now been nailed to the Cross—Around Him stood His executioners, the rough, unfeeling, Roman guards. He saw there before Him, His accusers—the mocking Pharisees and envious chief priests, all exulting over His downfall, as they thought. Beyond them are gathered the curious rabble, who had raised the cry of " Crucify Him ! " waiting in excitement for the next scene in this marvellous Drama. Perhaps there was a momentary hush among that strife of tongues, uttering railings and scoffing accusations against their victim, when Jesus lifts His eyes heavenward and pleads in love for these His enemies—" Father, forgive ; they know not what they do." What rich streams of mercy and compassion flowed in the purple of the Saviour's blood ! Forgetful of self—His own sufferings—calmly unheeding in His true patience and marvellous love, all the wrongs, affronts, contempts and cruel injustice offered by these His enemies. His one cry is for Forgiveness. Who can despair of pardon for sins committed, for work left undone, after such a scene ?—and with it comes the lesson—" Forgive thý brethren, even as I forgave thee."

The sorrowing friends of Jesus could not at first understand this pardon. Was it for this He lived ?—Was it for this He died ? Yes, for this, and more, O loving disciple, and faithful watcher. For your sins and mine the cry went forth, " Father, forgive them." Thus, when the allied powers of evil seemed to assail the Son of God, with the six dread

hours of coming agony before Him—with the crushing load
of the sin of mankind upon Him—with the harsh sounds of
His relentless foes clamouring around Him—the Saviour
breathed forgiveness in the first prayer of Calvary.

"Father!" Oh! how true a Son! See here the right
use of Prayer. That which was nearest to His great Heart
of Love escaped from His lips. He pleaded for pardon for
"All." Yes! Judas the betrayer—Pilate the fickle-minded—
Herod the sensual king—the narrow-minded priests and
prejudiced Pharisees—the hard-hearted soldiers, and the
fierce, angry mob—All were included in that petition of love.
And we too have a place in the heart of Jesus. For pardon
He still pleads for us. *Intercessor* and *Mediator* are words
dear to every sinner. We too may pray, believing—
feeling, that our poor petitions are presented to "*Our
Father*" through the pleading lips of Jesus, that grace and
pardon may be given. This thought surely gives a new
value to prayer—sheds a brighter light on our feeble efforts,
for Jesus is with us and for us, as we pray :—

> "For us to wicked men betrayed,
> Scourged, mocked, in purple robe arrayed,
> He bore the shameful Cross and death,
> For us at length gave up His breath."[1]

Do we make the full use of Prayer that we might do?
All are ready to use Intermittent Prayer, when some special
sorrow bends us, or some arrow of conviction probes the
conscience, yet how few of us use Habitual Prayer, that is
live—*a life of Prayer*. We know that "Prayer is the breath
of the soul." It is a breathing out of self, and a breathing
in of God. We cannot live without Prayer. Again, our

---

[1] Hymns A. & M., 173.

F

Prayers are often too selfish, only framed to take in our own needs. What about our brothers' souls? Jesus prayed not for Himself, to teach us the right use of intercessory prayer. We need more intercessions for the Church at home—abroad—for faithful and heathen; for those near and dear to us, and our enemies; for those who scoff and rail still at holy things; for the prejudiced, and hard-hearted, open sinners. All need our prayers.

Yet here is the difficulty. We feel that we have nothing in common with such as these. Forgiveness enters not into the framing of our petitions. We have been wronged, misjudged, set at nought, evil-entreated, misrepresented, by certain persons whom we still regard as our enemies, and we cannot frame a prayer of forgiveness for such as these. O! remember the rebuke of the penitent thief to his hardened companion, "Dost not thou fear God?"[1] Will not this question from the dying thief startle us into beholding our very condition? Dare we withhold from others that which we so earnestly seek from God? Shall we not rather pray with our dying Saviour, "Father, forgive them," and so ourselves find mercy and pardon in our cry for others. Our Elder Brother Jesus is our pattern here; we are indeed proud of Him as we humbly follow in His steps.

[1] S. Luke xxiii. 40.

III.

"Being reviled, we bless; being persecuted, we suffer it; being defamed, we intreat."—1 COR. IV. 12, 13.

AND now, let us try to grasp the full power of forgiveness as we kneel in silent prayer and meditation before God. Let us mention by name in secret to Jesus any whom we have not yet forgiven. Rather let us pray for them than for ourselves, for do we not thus lighten our own burden of guilt by dealing out pardon to others? The Holy Jesus has been so gentle and forbearing with us in the past. As He hung upon the Cross of Suffering He had nothing to ask forgiveness for. He had no sin, and so He by His stupendous offering of Love, in giving up Himself for the " sin of the whole world," is able to plead to the Father for us.

Therefore breathe forgiveness for all who may have wronged or injured you. Think of that brother or sister who has acted or spoken against you. You once loved them—trusted them—now they have forfeited that love and confidence by acting against you. It may be they have deceived, or even robbed you—taken away your good name or character, or wounded you with words of passion, and you have made up your minds never to forgive them. Undo all this, to-day! Upon your knees plead for them as you behold with the eye of faith the Sinless Sufferer looking upon His cruel foes; as you hear His sweet cry of mercy, " Father, forgive them, for they know not what they do." *We need daily pardon as we need daily bread.* Each day, alas, brings its own tale of wrong doing and omission. In our most solemn moments how greatly we desire to unlive

some of the sins of the past.   Yet how great is the Love *not
yet tried*.   God still invites us to come for mercy, but only
if we feel the need of it, and can show mercy to others.
The unforgiving dare not say the words he acts to others—
" Forgive me not." [1]

[2] " O, brothers ! the Outstretched Hands of Jesus dying
still can embrace us, though we seem to be so far from
Him.   None need feel that they are outside His loving
grasp."

" They know not what they do." [3] Was it indeed in
ignorance that our dear Lord's enemies acted ?   Yes ! for
blinded by self-will, and envy, they knew Him not.   All
along He was so misunderstood by them, His pure simple
life so contrasted with their worldly idea of a Messiah, that
they cast Him out : His plain truth convicted them, and
goaded them to reject Him, while they cried, " His blood
be upon us and upon our children." [4] Theirs was indeed a
false knowledge which blinded their very souls, so that they
were unable to discern in Him their Saviour.   His mighty
works—His tender words—His hours of incessant toil had
only resulted in gathering a few poor disciples around Him,
and these, with but one or two exceptions, " forsook Him
and fled." [5] Truly they knew Him not.   And we—do we
know Him? Will our life work—our daily service—proclaim
this truth ?   Only one voice on Calvary's mount possessed
courage sufficient to acknowledge Him.   How strange that
exclamation which broke from the lips of the Centurion
guard must have sounded to the multitudes surrounding
Him—" Truly this was the Son of God." [6] The faithful

[1] See Med., " The Life of Forgiveness," Part I.
[2] Williamson's " Outstretched Hands," p. 5.   [3] S. Luke xxiii. 34.
[4] S. Matt. xxvii. 25.   [5] S. Matt. xxvi. 56.   [6] S. Matt. xxvii. 54.

few gazing in mournful silence beneath the shadow of His Cross knew it—felt it—to be true, yet mystery crowding upon mystery made even their faith and hope waver, and only love remained to sustain them in their sorrow.

And so with us, How often have we been ashamed to know Jesus ? How often has the world commanded that we should disown Him, and we have obeyed, although conscience has whispered, Why ? How often, when called upon to choose between right and wrong, we have given way, and the opportunity has fled never to return ? How many around us—in our midst still know Him not, but rank themselves with the multitude against Him, spending the solemn hours of each returning Lent and Good Friday in worldly pleasure and sensual excess, while the cry of the suffering Redeemer still pleads for their salvation : " Father, forgive them, for they know not what they do."[1] Let us give them a place in our petitions : *For to know Him is to love Him, and to adore Him for ever. Amen.*

[1] S. Luke xxiii. 34.

THE PENITENT'S WELCOME.
I.

SECOND WORD.

"Verily I say unto thee—To-day shalt thou be with Me in Paradise."
—S. LUKE XXIII. 43.

AISE thine eyes to Jesus Crucified, and see if there be any sorrow like unto His sorrow? Doth not His very silence plead :

[1] " Is it nothing to you all ye that pass by ?
For you I suffer, for you I die.
Oh ! men and women, your deeds of shame,
Your sins without reason, and number, and name,
I bear them all on the Cross on high ;
Is it nothing to you all ye that pass by ? "

Meditate, once again, upon the wild scene of confusion surrounding the Cross. The air is filled with a babel of human voices clamouring against that Sinless Sufferer, or mocking and insulting Him as He appears in love to draw all men unto Himself. His sacred Hands are still stretched out in blessing, yet they are pierced with the cruel nails ; His holy brow bears the crown of thorns ; His exposed body, mangled and torn, shows forth the perfect *Image of God* restored in Suffering Man. There behold Him put to open shame, derided, hanging between two condemned malefactors like a common criminal. His very companions in death actually railing against Him. " They that were crucified with Him reviled Him."[2] So the truth flashes

[1] Stainer's Crucifixion—"The Appeal of the Crucifix," p. 50.
[2] S. Mark xv. 32.

across my soul—Even that poor, desolate, insulted Sufferer was " My Lord and My God." [1]

Oh ! Sacred Mystery ! Oh ! Divine Fount of Love, to move Thee, my precious Saviour, to die for me, even me ! What can I render to Thee for all Thou hast borne and suffered for me ?

This is indeed a solemn scene to meditate upon. Two long, weary hours of agonising pain have passed. But one word has hitherto escaped from the patient lips of Jesus, and that an earnest prayer for His enemies, even while they nailed Him to the Cross—" Father, forgive them;" for He Who suffered was the Lord of Life—the Immortal, Infinite God, Who at this very moment supplied these His ruthless enemies with life and breath and all things. If but for one moment His care had been withdrawn, their breath had ceased, though :—" Still soldiers mock and Jews deride " Him, not believing in His power. Tired and weary of their cruel work of torture, with their throats hoarse from those loud cries of calumny and shame, the hard-hearted soldier guards fling themselves upon the ground to watch their Victim, wondering no doubt at His patient silence ; while ever and anon they cast careless and indifferent glances upon the increasing crowd of scoffing priests and elders mingling among the excited mob, whom they have incited to fury in their wild cries of " He trusted in God that He would deliver Him ; Let Him deliver Him now if He will have Him, for He said, I am the Son of God," [2] and that more bitter saying of, " He saved others ; Himself He cannot save. Let Him come down now from the Cross, and we will believe in Him." [3]

No, the dear dying Saviour could not save Himself, for

[1] S. John xx. 28.   [2] S. Matt. xxvii. 43.   [3] S. Matt. xxvii. 42.

Golden -

Bishop Paddock ...

had He not willed to *save us*, and the full penalty of death
was His to bear that we might live through Him? So
no answer is vouchsafed to their words, which surge around
the Cross as a final storm of mockery, hatred, and scornful
malice. They had brought about His death. Was not this
sufficient to staunch their envy? No! still they cry, while
the suffering Saviour beholds their final efforts to overcome
Him, as with bowed Head He seeks to bear the very sins
they are committing against Him.

II.

"To-day shalt thou be with Me in Paradise."—S. LUKE XXIII. 43.

NOW we may imagine a second short lull in the
noise of the crowd. Just a few moments of calm
after the fierce tempest of evil sayings. It may
be now that the two malefactors look at their
Fellow-Sufferer. Both hitherto had joined in the bitter
cry of the multitude against Him, but the calm dignity of
that Bruised Face—the holy patience of that Sinless One—
the noble endurance of pain, ignominy, and cruel shame
during the past two hours of suffering have at last done their
work. The heart of Dysmas (for so he hath been called)
hath been touched by the grace and love of his Redeemer.
The Good Shepherd hath not sought in vain for the wandering sheep, and Oh! Glad Tidings of great joy!—He is even
now about to bear it home in triumph to His Father's Fold.

Mark the marvellous change in that pale, suffering frame
of the penitent thief. The fire of anger hath left his eye—
the voice of railing and scorn is for ever hushed—the proud
spirit of evil is quenched—the hardened heart of long years

of sin is at last softened, melted, crushed and broken beneath the loving rays of the Sun of Righteousness. The robber is saved, caught back from the precipice of eternal destruction and death, by the loving, strong arms of that Saviour he has but so lately reviled. Won by His great Heart of Love, that poor dying thief, who for long years past, nay, perhaps through a very lifetime, has resisted grace, at last has found his Redeemer and Friend in the person of his once despised Fellow-Sufferer. What then is his first act upon coming to himself? What can he now do to show his new love and prove his gratitude to his Saviour? Oh! marvellous change! So lately a railer, now he seeks to be a preacher of salvation to his brother's soul. Listen to his voice as earnestly—sincerely, he addresses his robber companion, who still seeks to forget his own sufferings by reviling and cursing the Holy Son of God. " Dost thou not fear God, seeing thou art in the same condemnation, and we, indeed justly, for the due reward of our deeds, but this Man hath done nothing amiss."[1] So would he lead that old companion and brother in guilt to his dying Redeemer hanging at his side, there to offer his sin-burdened soul for pardon and grace, ere it be too late. Then with a bright ray of hope spread over his countenance, he turns once more to the Face of the Saviour for sympathy and help, as he pours out his one true prayer of penitence, " Lord (Master), remember me when Thou comest into Thy Kingdom."[2]

Was He a King, then? Yes! though crowned with thorns of suffering, and His Throne but the Tree of Shame, yet His Kingly power and majesty asserted itself, and the Cross ever shines forth as the Tree of Glory—The True Tree of Life whose " fruits are for the healing of all people." The

[1] S. Luke xxiii. 40, 41.   [2] S. Luke xxiii. 42.

King shall not return to His kingdom alone, for one true
subject hath been called to accompany Him, though that
subject be but a poor penitent robber. That prayer of
Dysmas could not be prayed in vain. That deep, heartfelt
pleading could not but find a quick and full response in the
Saviour's dying Heart of mercy. A soul won :—the first
fruits of the Cross :—a foretaste of victory in His hour of
shame and suffering :—a penitent brought home. Truly
were those words fulfilled, " If I, even I, be lifted up, I
will draw all men unto Me,"[1] when the gracious answer
came to that earnest, pleading soul, " To-day shalt thou be
with Me in Paradise."[2] Pain and suffering ended : all
trials over ; peace, joy, and rest eternal in My presence ;
with Me in Paradise to learn to know and to love Me well,
that thou mayest hereafter dwell with Me for ever in
Heaven. " Well done, thou good and faithful servant :
enter thou into the joy of thy Lord."[3]

Oh brothers, what a marvellous message of salvation breaks
upon our ears, " A broken and contrite heart, O God, Thou
wilt not despise."[4] The penitent confesses his past sins to
his Saviour : he cries for mercy, yet asks for no relief from
present suffering—for that suffering hath brought him to Jesus.
Now he can but count his cross but gain in company with
his dear Lord. Having once found, his only fear is separation from his King, so he craves for a place in His Kingdom
of Love ; he longs for the companionship of His new Master,
through and beyond the dark valley which is even now
opening out before him. This is true penitence, and then,
O sweetest answer of Divine compassion ! What wonderful condescension for Thou, O my Jesus, to stoop so low as

---

[1] S. John xii. 32.   [2] S. Luke xxiii. 43.   [3] S. Matt. xxv. 21.
[4] Ps. li. 17.

to care for me : to promise to me, a poor, worthless sinner, so much grace and life eternal : to offer in Thy fulness of love, much more than I can ever dare to ask of Thee. " To-day," not hereafter only—A present blessing—not remembrance only, but Thine ever-abiding Presence. Jesus with me, even in the dark valley of Death : Jesus still my companion in the Paradise of God :—Thus the Holy Redeemer spake to the penitent thief—Thus my loving Master and Saviour speaks to-day to my soul.

III.

" To-day shalt thou be with Me in Paradise."—S. LUKE XXIII. 43.

> "O come unto Me ! This awful price,
> Redemption's tremendous sacrifice,
> Is paid for you. Oh! why will ye die?
> Is it nothing to you, all ye that pass by? " [1]

HAT individual application do I find here ?   Have I wilfully rejected Him hitherto in the past ? Have all His pleadings with me been in vain ? Have I ever railed in open rebellion against my God ?   Do I this day earnestly desire His presence ?   To be with Him, where He is ?   If so, I must also be ready to suffer.   " Are ye able to drink of the cup that I shall drink of ?   To be baptized with the baptism that I am baptized with ? " [2] the Saviour still asks of His disciples.

" No cross, no crown," is the Master's rule, for the present shame and suffering shall reveal the future glory and rest in the presence of my God.   How many thoughts arise upon this second word of pardon from the Cross.   See the

---

[1] Stainer's Crucifixion, p. 54.   [2] S. Matt. xx. 22.

bountiful goodness, love, and mercy of Jesus to the penitent thief. He asked simply for remembrance—not to be forgotten, when Jesus should come to His Kingdom; and lo! He promised him that Kingdom; He looked upon him, and loved him, and in compassion He raised that poor fallen one from his degradation and suffering to peace and glory. He forgave all his sins, and promised Paradise.

Mark how the Sinless One forgets His own sufferings to listen to a sinner's cry for mercy. He is silent when maledictions are poured upon Him by an angry crowd, but as soon as the pleading voice of one poor sufferer catches His ear, He *turns* towards him and claims him as His own.

Again, what marvellous love towards Him should this act of Jesus awake in my heart. Oh! that tale of sin which is so closely woven into my life's history—that dreadful barrier that I have been building around me to keep God out of my thoughts and ways: that love of self-will, disobedience, sloth, selfish ease, and worldliness, which have throughout been my burden instead of the dear Master's yoke of self-sacrifice. The wrongs I have committed by example: The souls I have ruined: The evil I have wilfully done to others: the trouble, misery, and sorrow I have caused in my home circle: those hours of idleness or luxury, in which God was forgotten: those neglected Communions, and thoughtless acts of prayer: those despised means of grace. Can I also with the remembrance of such a catalogue of misdoing and neglect, plead for forgiveness from my dearest Lord? Have I a place still in that great Heart of Love? Does He still care for me?—Even me? Listen to His voice. To-day shalt thou, even thou, be with Me—forgiven, pardoned, cleansed, healed, strengthened, comforted, and My ever-abiding presence shall indeed be a Paradise to thee,

for " Lo! I am with thee, always, even unto the end."[1]
One thing I would require of thee : Take up the cross and
bear it after Me—Prove your love for Me before men by
showing your true discipleship—your readiness to suffer in
the noble cause of right : confess Me, faithfully as My true
soldier and servant : keep true to your Baptismal vows.
Trust Me more. Make Me thine own. Confide in Me
to-day and for ever, and " Take My yoke, learn of Me, and
ye shall find rest to your souls."[2] Be strong : be pure : be
holy : be bold to rebuke evil. Come thou and tell Me all
thy grief, child of My love! Then may we answer :—

> " Let but the cross on which I bleed,
>   Stand, Jesus, near to Thine—
> Then in my sorest hour of need
>   Thy Heart shall speak to mine;
> My cross shall keep me near to Thee,
>   While evil in me dies ;
> Thy Cross at last shall set me free
>   To pass to Paradise." *Anon.*[3]

[1] S. Matt. xxviii. 20.   [2] S. Matt. xi. 29.
         [3] "The Daily Round," p. 140.

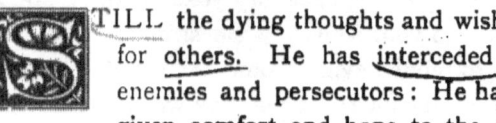

THE MOTHER AND THE BELOVED
DISCIPLE.

I.

THIRD WORD.

"Woman, behold thy son—Behold thy mother."—S. JOHN XIX. 26, 27.

STILL the dying thoughts and wishes of Jesus are for others. He has interceded for His cruel enemies and persecutors : He has pardoned and given comfort and hope to the dying robber at His side, and now He commends His mother to the care of His beloved disciple, S. John. So Jesus would teach us in His death, as in His life, filial obedience and love. O, what a noble example to follow :

> " A Son that never did amiss,
> That never shamed His mother's kiss,
>   Nor crossed her fondest prayer ;
> E'en from the Cross He deigned to bow,
> For her His agonizèd Brow,
>   Still His sole earthly care." *Anon.*

Thus the Saviour entirely put aside His own agonies, His sacred thoughts went back to the sweet simplicity and purity of the old Home Life at Nazareth, with His gentle, loving mother as the central figure there. Now, that dear mother is bowed down with grief, for the prophecy of the aged Simeon hath overtaken her—"A sword shall pierce through thine own soul also."[1] Jesus knew all this. He fully understood the great love of a mother, and in His dying accents He blended it with a pure unfathomable love

[1] S. Luke ii. 35.

that could not be silent, but proclaimed its power in those sweet words, " Behold thy son." [1]

How close to us the Divine Master comes, when in His dying hours—in his manly heart of love—He unites His Mother to His friend and chosen disciple.   How sweet in God's sight is true friendship !   How valued among men !   In His hour of great conflict the willing Sufferer—thy God and mine, cares for those on earth, those nearest and dearest to Him.   So we would gather around our dying bed, the friends we love the best.   When the old way hath been trodden, and the unknown path lies before us ; when the old life is fast ebbing away, and the new life is dawning before us, it is our friends, our loved ones, and, best of all, a mother that we look for to comfort us while we express our loving farewells, and make plans for their future happiness.   So the household, knit together by the firm bonds of love, faith, and hope, is the true family of Jesus.   [2] " How He, my dearest Saviour, hallowed the common ties of kindred and affection.   He wills to bind those who love Him in holy friendship.   He wills to make each Christian home on this Day of days like that which, in obedience to Him, S. Mary and S. John shared together."   And what a true sequel to the dying command of his Master we find—" And from that hour that disciple took her unto his own home." [3]   Both recognised the sacred charge committed to them.   Obedience was full and perfect, and Love prevailed.   What a rich reward was this third saying of Jesus to those faithful souls, whose great love gave them courage (while others hid themselves, or but ventured to stand afar off) to hear themselves addressed in this way.   As the patient, sorrow-stricken Mother grasps the full truth that the world's salvation is being won by that dear Sufferer

[1] S. John xix. 26.   [2] " Daily Round," p. 141.   [3] S. John xix. 27.

Who looks down from His Cross of pain upon her, think you not that her thoughts went not back to the manger cradle of that first Christmas morn, when He, as a helpless Babe, looked up from His humble bed and smiled upon her. What a life of innocence, self-sacrifice, and love was linked together by these two events in the minds of both Mother and Son. The sacred scenes of the cottage home at Nazareth all rose up in succession to teach the life of perfect obedience and willing self-sacrifice, now fast ebbing away as that precious Blood flowed for the sins of all mankind. Yes, the loving Mother understood now that she must resign her Son. She no doubt longed to minister to His intense sufferings—to alleviate those death agonies by the loving caress of a mother's kiss—to support Him, or gently soothe His pain in her tender arms. Yet, No! it cannot, may not be; His cup of suffering, even to the bitter dregs of death, He wills to drain alone. So did the Saviour fulfil the prediction, " I have trodden the wine-press alone; and of the people there was none with Me." [1]

II.

" Woman, behold thy son—Behold thy mother."—S. JOHN XIX. 26, 27.

HOME! Sweet word, still living in the Heart of Jesus, to make Him for a few moments forget His Cross and sufferings. At Home He was known — beloved — understood. From Calvary, my dearest brothers and sisters, flows the pure, unfailing stream which quickens and strengthens the home life. There the True Example pleads with parents and children in those

[1] Is. lxiii. 3.

dying accents, " Behold thy son—behold thy mother."
There it is that the indissoluble knot of Christian love—
family unity—is made by Jesus. Oh, parents, see to your
homes. The Cross demands it. Jesus pleads for it. Make
your homes such as He would like them to be—bright,
happy places. The brightest gems are said to be, " *Mother,
Home, and Heaven.*" What about the first two of these?
They are in our own making. The Home Life reveals us
as we really are. There we put aside restraint : We are at
least natural there, when shielded from the gaze of men
and women whose criticism we fear, or whose good opinion
we are not prepared to forfeit. In the Home we doff our
garb of outward unreality, and too often, alas ! the smooth
tongue becomes snappish and hurtful, or the mask of
amiability falls from us, but to reveal fretful discontent,
and even malicious feeling towards others.

When you meditate upon this, ask yourselves, What
must the Home of Nazareth have been like ?—What that
Home where S. John and the Mother of our dear Lord
dwelt ? Home, to be worthy of that name at all, should
be a Fount of purity : a Rock from which the true manhood
may be hewn : The Anchor around which the family feel
safely fixed : The happiest, holiest spot on earth, where
our Jesus deigns to come to sanctify our efforts and to
bring light, and peace, and love to all therein.

Yet what sad scenes are revealed to us ! Mothers crushed
down by the bad conduct and waywardness of sons and
daughters. "Her boy," "Her girl," steeped in shame and
degradation, whose names held in honour would light up
that mother's eyes with joy and just pride, and make her
breast throb with happiness for their welfare. Fathers—
Husbands ! here also is a lesson for us. Ours it is to bear

G

a share of the home troubles and worries. We sometimes are stumbling-blocks, or tyrants, demanding submission in the home circle. Yet our Blessed Lord committed to S. John His mother. He was to be her support and protector. Are we all this? Not in the perfunctory routine of bread-winners only, but in spiritual matters? Our privilege and vocation is to be the protector from evil of those gentler inmates of the home—the patient, loving wife, and the tender children: To be the guide in all holiness, purity, and truth. Our example can alone teach Manliness, Religion, Faith, and Duty to those depending upon us. What are we doing here? The dying Saviour pleads for our portion of Life Service in the Home Circle.

III.

"Woman, behold thy son —Behold thy mother."—S. JOHN XIX. 26. 27.

IN reverence we may ask the motive of Jesus in commending His Mother to S. John's protecting care. She was, undoubtedly, alone in the world, as Holy Scripture is silent about her husband. "Joseph the carpenter," was already dead, and thus was this shelter provided for her. It was a task given to the disciple to test his love and obedience. Again, may not the Holy Jesus have desired to remove the feeling of utter loneliness from His Mother's heart, as He knew that the continued sight of His great sufferings were too much for her. The Hand she had kissed in Infancy :—the Hand she had guided and led in Childhood :—the Hand that had even ministered to her needs through life—now pointed in death to the new Home, with

its new ties and duties, in company with the beloved disciple.
So Jesus transfers the duties hitherto performed by Himself
to His trusted followers, the Apostles of His Church, into
which we have been admitted by the Sacrament of Holy
Baptism. This Church entrusted to His faithful Apostles
is in our keeping, even as we are in Its keeping. United,
bound together, in ties of holy friendship—kinship—even as
we are members of Christ, children of God, and inheritors
of that future Kingdom of Glory.

And then, what a noble example of compassion and care for
the sorrow and needs of others we have here. The wounded
heart of grief of our dear Lord's Mother, and the genuine
sorrow of His beloved disciple, surmounted His own grief and
suffering, and He sought only to comfort them. Are we His
true disciples in this sense ? Are we all engaged in helping
others ? or are we in our selfish indulgence only able to
think about, and to brood over our own trials and sufferings ?
What does the voice of your dying Saviour say ? " Behold
thy mother—behold thy son! "[1] Oh! those multitudes of
men and women bowed down beneath their various burdens
of sin, suffering, anguish sore, and bodily discomfort.
Behold them—and beholding, stretch out the hand of
succour, bid the cold heart go out to them, to feel for
their distress, and so feeling, to help them. There may
be ignorance, needing the light of your knowledge ; sickness and want may be so placed at your gate by God, as an
opportunity for you to show your true discipleship—" Inasmuch as ye have done it to the least of these, My brethren,
ye have done it unto Me,"[2] saith the Master still, and
this hallows your deeds of mercy and love to His service.
Of your charity be bountiful to the needs of God's Church—

[1] S. John xix. 26, 27.   [2] S. Matt. xxv. 40.

her mission fields, her home labours, her services, her children.   Remember it was to S. John, whose loving care it was given to provide a home for his dear Lord's mother, that the bright vision of the New Home of Heaven was given.   " I, John, saw the Holy City, New Jerusalem, coming down from God, out of Heaven, prepared as a bride adorned for her husband."[1]   In our next pause for silent prayer beneath the shadow of His Cross, let us ask for grace to minister to the needs of others.   There is a soul somewhere, perhaps in the home circle, some waif of earth, needing our friendly hand of guidance.   There are many sorrows—many tears around us—to wipe away in God's dear name.   There may be bitterness to soothe, anger to calm, even among those near and dear to us.   There is a broken heart for us to bind up, a crushed life to raise up, and to point to that Lone Figure Who still by His bitter Death seeks to draw all men unto Himself, by His crowning act of love and sacrifice.   And what more glorious passport to the Home above can there be than those simple words, " He brought them to Jesus " ?

[1] Rev. xxi. 2.

4 a. m.

THE LONELY SUFFERER.

I.

FOURTH WORD.

" My God, My God, why hast Thou forsaken Me? "

—S. MATT. XXVII. 46.

O back with me in thought to another distant scene. It is a fair and beautiful garden, where man in his pristine beauty communed daily in some mysterious way with his God and Father. Yet as we gaze upon the bright scene a sad change appears, even as a blight to blot out that Paradise of Love. The beauty of holiness suddenly fades from Adam's brow, his eyes, once so bright and expectant, have now lost their lustre, and they are filled with sadness. The head but lately raised Heavenward is now downcast through shame and consciousness of evil done. Lo! our first parents seek for shelter among the rich foliage of Paradise. Shame and fear make them crouch as they attempt to hide from that God Whom hitherto they have sought for, and talked with, as their only Father and Friend. Disobedience appears as the first sin to do its sad work. Satan has stepped in to estrange man from his Creator. It is the sad story of The Fall from holiness to ruin, and degradation, and death. In deepest love, in tenderest pity, yet in righteous anger did the Almighty and Omniscient Father seek His children. " Adam, where art thou? "[1] Child of My Creation—Son of My Heart, what hast thou done? The very Voice of God breathed sorrow for the lost ones, as they wandered from His presence in the paths of disobedience and self-will.

[1] Gen. iii. 9.

And this scene with all its dire results fades away into the sterner picture of The Sacrifice on Calvary. There we behold our crucified Redeemer paying back the penalty in all its bitter reality and fulness ; there we see Him wiping out alone the misery of sin which brought this separation from God. Behold the true Burden-bearer of all ;—atoning for every act of wilful sin in all ages, past, present, and future.

Thus the Divine Master, Jesus, stemmed alone the mighty torrent of evil, as a suffering, though a sinless, Conqueror. Oh! that word *Alone !* How much desolation it brought upon the soul of the forsaken Son of God. There the Willing Victim, hanging between Heaven and earth, a spectacle before men and angels, in solitary suffering and bitter anguish, was alone—deserted—deprived of all Divine assistance. Yes, even the Father's Face of love is averted— the Father's Hand of support is withdrawn, during those dark, shadowy moments of sacrifice for the sin of a lost world. No wonder our dear Lord expressed His extreme agony in the bitter cry, " My God! My God! why hast Thou for- saken Me ? "[1] His spirit pleaded in its desolation— " Hitherto I have had Thee, O My Father, by My side, as a Refuge ; a Stronghold whereunto I might always resort."[2] Thy " great love hath hitherto encompassed Me on every side ; Thy presence cheered and supported Me ; but now, even now, in My hour of greatest need, dost Thou, Oh, My Father, withdraw Thyself from Thy Beloved Son."

Yes, brothers, the last pillow of support is withdrawn from the Head of Jesus, "and the full flood of desolation rushes in upon *the Forsaken One*, as the Passion reaches its climax when the Face of the Father is withdrawn from

[1] S. Matt. xxvii. 46.   [2] Psalm lxxi. 3.

Him. The darkness of nature does but symbolise the thick darkness in which His Soul is wrapped; and out of the deep of that impenetrable loneliness the cry goes to Heaven, ' My God! My God! why hast Thou forsaken Me?'[1] The consolations of Deity, which had hitherto sustained Him, are suddenly cut off; the desertion of man had been hard to bear, to be forsaken of God was intolerable. . . . His sufferings are for a moment absolutely without relief from man or God."[2] What a marvellous response rolls over the past ages to that searching question of the Father, " Adam, where art Thou?"[3] do we find in this death-cry of Jesus, the Second Adam, " Who was the Son of God." Yet how closely bound together are " the sowing and the harvest of evil." Man, lost to God by disobedience in Eden, hath been redeemed to God by the entire submission of the Saviour's Will.

" When we behold Thy bleeding wounds, and the rough way that
    Thou hast trod,
Make us to hate the load of sin that lay so heavy on our God."
                                  Anon.

II.

" My God, My God, why hast Thou forsaken Me?"—PSALM XXII. 1.

E have been watching near the Cross of Jesus each day during this holy season. Are we getting weary, tired of remaining in His presence? If so, let us pray for more devotion—for an increase of spiritual zeal and fervour—for an outpouring of love from on high—for that presence of our God and Father which was denied to our dear Master.

Why have we undertaken this Lenten Meditation? Why

[1] S. Matt. xxvii. 46.   [2] " The Sinless Sufferer," p. 64.   [3] Gen. iii. 9.

have we been more regular at Holy Communion and at the
daily Services during this Holy Season ? Are we prepared
to answer this question ? Is it curiosity, or the mere
novelty of this special season, that have attracted us within
the sacred walls. If so, God grant that any who may have
gone to see may be led to remain to watch and pray.
Again, do we go to please others, or because others are
there ? If so, may we so learn the deep—deep truth of the
story of the Cross, and feel our own need of that Precious
Blood-shedding to cleanse, revive, and save our guilty, sin-
stricken souls. Let us remember that the Cross of Jesus is
the Only Teacher at this time. Our part is to meditate and
adore. We would find Jesus only. We would watch with
Him in His hour of loneliness. We desire to offer to Him
to-day :

> " A broken heart, a fount of tears,
> Ask, and they will not be denied ;
> Lord Jesus, may we love and weep,
> Since Thou for us art crucified." [1]

[2] " It was about the ninth hour of the day. During the
last three hours Jesus had been hanging on the Cross in
silence and darkness ; what He suffered—what He felt and
thought—we can never know ; but we do know that our
pardon, our life, our hope, depends upon what He was
doing. Those were the precious moments in which He
made Atonement for our sins." How true, then, that railing
cry of the chief priests, " He saved others, Himself He
cannot save." [3] No ! not save Himself, else where would
my redemption be ? Who then would pay the penalty for

---

[1] Hymns A. & M. 114, v. 6.
[2] " Practical Reflections on the Holy Gospels," p. 173.
[3] S. Matt. xxvii. 42.

my sins? No! that Love which passeth knowledge, pure, holy, mysterious, Heavenly Love led my Jesus to suffer in silence and gloom ; while earth's powers were shaken, as they refused to appear before such a solemn Sacrifice.

The end was rapidly approaching. The battle was even now being won while the Cross of the Victor was shrouded in thick darkness, and silence deep and still reigned around. The angry and malicious crowd are at last silenced; their mocking tongues are hushed; the penitent thief can no longer discern his Master's Face through the gloom; the faithful mourners have now probably left the Cross ; gently and tenderly the sorrowing Mother has suffered herself to be led to her new home, in obedience to her Saviour's words of commendation. But what remains? Fear and trembling now seize the bystanders, as denser—darker grows the veil. What do Pilate and Herod think now? What do the Chief Priests feel, as the preparation for the Passover is hindered ? This Miracle of miracles affects all, and the terror-stricken multitudes are silenced.

And may not we in this dread silence enquire of that Lone Figure now hidden from us, What is this? It is surely the dark, angry cloud of sin enveloping the Lord of Light. The battle is hidden from human eyes. And the keenest struggle comes with the separation from the Father. [1] " Yes, marvellous thought ! God, Who beheld in Jesus the Man laden with all the iniquities of the human race, forsook Him, and left Him without support or consolation to these fearful sufferings of soul and body. Hence His bitter cry, *My God, My God, why hast Thou forsaken Me ?* [2] May not the earnest soul enquire, " What have I done, O Lord, that Thou shouldest bestow any Heavenly comfort upon me ?

[1] " Nourishment of the Christian Soul," p. 345.   [2] " Imitation of Christ."

I am not worthy of Thy consolation, nor of any spiritual visitation. Nay, I am not even worthy of the least comfort in my hour of trial and sorrow, yet I know that a contrite and humble heart Thou canst not despise."

III.

" Out of the deep have I called unto Thee, O Lord ; Lord, hear my voice."—PSALM CXXX. 1 *(P.B. Version)*.

E have seen throughout how our dear Lord's Passion far exceeded all human suffering, by reason of its utter loneliness. All through that Spotless Life on earth He dwelt among men, yet not of men. He was so far separated from them, for He, Omniscient, was surrounded by ignorance ; He, the All-holy, by sin ; He, the Almighty, by human weakness—and now in death " He looks for some to have pity upon Him ; but there is no man, neither finds He any to comfort Him." [1]

And so, in a less degree, surely we must pass through life alone. One by one we are born into the world ; one by one we must leave it. Yes, though we be surrounded by loving friends—we are *alone*—individuals in a crowd—in the home circle—in the brotherhood. We possess many common ties, we may have much common thought and kindred feelings, yet we still remain as units, and " the heart alone knoweth its own bitterness ; " [2] while the soul alone discerneth its own trials, failings, short-comings, and burdens.

Hath God our Father gently laid the Cross of Solitude upon us ? Oh, remember how keenly, bitterly, it bowed down the Lord Jesus, and so learn to bear it for His dear sake.

---

[1] Psalm lxix. 20 *(P.B. Version)*.   [2] Prov. xiv. 10.

However lonely, desolate, outcast, misunderstood by men we may be, God is still with us. [1] "God never wholly forsakes us. We could not bear it." We can never realize that feeling of our Master, when our sins—your sins and mine—blotted out the Father's presence during His dying moments. I know repeated acts of wilful sin will separate the soul from its Creator, but even then the Father's voice in love and sorrow asks, " Where art Thou ? " and Jesus, the true Shepherd, still follows the wandering soul, to save it, saying, " Come unto Me . . . . I will give you rest." [2]

With the Master's promise we cannot be forsaken. Death may rob us of all we hold near and dear on earth. The aching void may proclaim our loss, yet God is near to calm the heaving breast, and bid the troubled spirit rest by His word, "Peace ! be still." [3] And should the world rob me of all I possess, then like the Christian martyr of other days, I will answer: " When all hath been taken from me, then will I cling the closer to my God."

Again, we must pray to realize the presence of Jesus to succour us in our times of Worship. His Sacred Presence can alone bring peace and grace in our acts of devotion. He must be with us to sanctify each offering of body, soul, and spirit to our Father. Through Him alone have we redemption. Through Him alone are our prayers and sacraments accepted. Do we find Him really in our cry for mercy and grace, or are we self-satisfied, and so make our worship unreal by not feeling the need of our Jesus ? Jesus hath sanctified suffering, therefore it is a sign of love. As we patiently bear bodily, mental or spiritual suffering, we are drawn closer and closer to His

[1] " The Sinless Sufferer," p. 72.   [2] S. Matt. xi. 29, 30.
[3] S. Mark iv. 39.

Cross. We feel the greater need of His presence, as our own helplessness becomes more apparent. As one by one the dark clouds of earth's night gather around us, we strain our eyes the more to catch the first bright streak of the dawn which lights up the shores of Paradise.

> "Lord, should fear and anguish roll
> Darkly on my sinful soul,
> Thou Who once was thus bereft
> That Thine own might ne'er be left,
> Teach me, by that bitter cry,
> In the gloom to know Thee nigh." [1]

ATHIRST.

I.

FIFTH WORD.

"I thirst."—S. JOHN XIX. 28.

"IN Jesus crucified there is an unveiling of God," therefore the sinner breathes Hope. As the poor drooping souls look up half ashamed, half dazed at that wondrous Sacrifice for them, they for the first time perhaps realize the bright and glorious truth that forgiveness is at hand. Even "Hope" for the penitent, which maketh not ashamed, and as they realize this glorious hope, the Past is recalled with all its vast trail of evil done and work left undone ; disobedience on the one hand—sloth and indifference on the other ; then the Present crowds forward, and the Present, which is so intense—narrow —limited—is so seldom used as God would have it used ; and lastly, the unknown misty Future appears, not so dark

[1] Hymns A. & M., 118, v. 5.

as hitherto, because the light of Jesus' Passion falls upon it. In that Sacrifice there is a life-giving power to unmake the past. This is Hope—for with Unbelief there is no Hope—no ray of Salvation to beckon onward—without the Cross all is dark.

We have seen " that Lonely Sufferer to be our God," and His Cross of suffering glorified, beautified, with its Sacred Burden now reveals to us the Throne of our King, from which Jesus reigned triumphant in suffering. The Altar of our High Priest upon which He offered Himself, " a full, perfect, and sufficient Sacrifice, Oblation, and Satisfaction for the sins of the whole world."[1] The Tribunal of our Judge, where He appears to separate the good from the evil. The Mercy-seat of our God before which we cry for pardon. The Trophy of our Victor whereby we are saved. The Ensign of the Captain of our Salvation, Whose Cross we bear, in His Name and for His dear Sake. So we believe, while Faith begets Hope and enkindles Love towards our dear suffering Lord, " Who became sin for us," and died that we might live.

" After this," says S. John, referring to the Saviour's last duty to His Mother, " Jesus knowing that all things were now accomplished, that the Scripture might be fulfilled, saith, ' I thirst.' Now there was a vessel set there full of vinegar ; and they filled a sponge with vinegar, and put on it hyssop, and applied it to His mouth."[2]

How these little details teach the perfection of God's law. The sacred Hyssop of purification made use of in the Jewish sacrifices; dipped in the blood of the bird in cleansing the leper ; and the instrument marking the lintel and door-posts with the blood of the Paschal Lamb in Egypt, is now used

[1] Prayer for the Church Militant.   [2] S. John xix. 28, 29.

in the Consummation of the Great Atonement—when the
Sacrifice of Love is finished—when the final Purification for
sin is made.

The Fifth Word again proves the perfect humanity of
Jesus. It is God's law that the sin of the body brings
suffering. So the Sinless One cried out in His parched,
bodily suffering. The weariness of pain was felt. Exhaustion had commenced. The preliminary burning throat and
dried lips proved it. Jesus was so like us, and yet so unlike
in His suffering. He truly grasped the perfect law of
suffering. He uttered no heedless cry. He reasoned it all
out, yet shrank not from its bitterness. The Scripture was
fulfilled in this death-cry. How blessed and good, because
in this word, " I thirst," our dear Lord appealed to men—
even to us. We can minister to His needs. In our suffering we need His help. Now He shows He needs our
sympathy. He is a fellow-sufferer. And yet not so,
brothers, for He is indeed suffering in our stead. It is all
so pure and beautiful. Does Jesus need our ministrations
now? Yes! Are we not too emotional in our service?
too forgetful? All prayer, all crying for mercy—too little
ministering. Our lives are not balanced rightly. This cry
reminds us of work to do around us for Jesus—To aid
others in His Name—to alleviate suffering for His Sake.
We dare not refuse, when we meditate upon the Thirst
of the pure soul of our God. That strong yearning which
nothing could satisfy short of the passion for those souls
dead and lost to Him. So the Master cries, " I thirst."
Give me thine Heart ! Life for Life. Love for Love. O,
brothers, do not be indifferent—cold—any more. Remember
that for our souls, our salvation He thirsts still.

It is a spiritual strain to think so long upon Jesus.

Hearts grow faint and souls thirst. O ! Jesus, take us just as we are. We offer ourselves to Thee—tired—wicked— unworthy—to quench Thy Thirst of Love.

II.

"Je~us saith, I thirst."—S. JOHN XIX. 28.

THE darkness is now past and over. The light of the Father's presence has again returned. The Victor comes faint from the dark strife, and as the spiritual conflict closes, He cries in His exhaustion, "I thirst." O, those sweet words of the Psalmist : "My soul thirsteth for God, for the living God : when shall I come and appear before God ? "[1]

What a suitable refrain to the thirsty cry of the Saviour for the souls of men. It is not easy for us to believe that there is within us anything that God loves so much that He wishes to possess it, and dwell there. It is one of God's mysteries. You remember the old, old story of Jacob's Well, how Jesus thirsted for the life-devotion and service of that poor sin-laden woman of Samaria, when He asked her to give Him to drink. How gently, tenderly, He unfolded her life of wrong-doing, to make her feel the need of that Living Water which He alone could give. And so now. The appeal from the Cross is full of tender- ness. He is the true "Horeb" smitten for us in the wilderness of this world. Yet He asks for something in return, nay, He craves, He thirsts for thine heart and mine. He cries :—

" My life was given for thee,
What hast thou given to Me? "[2]

[1] Ps. xlii. 2.   [2] Miss Havergal.

Shall we not bring Him all that we possess—ourselves—
our souls and bodies—and lay them at His Cross?   The
vigour and best of life, not the dregs of our days, or the
worthless lees of a mis-spent existence.

[1]" From the hot furnace of His sufferings He asks me
to give Him to drink."   Shall I let be, as if I cared not,
and refuse the refreshment He pleads for ?   I can comfort
Him by thirsting for God, and for His righteousness.   He
longs to refresh and cheer me with His grace, till I am
satisfied in His presence, and "thirst no more for ever."
And the question—the great question, is, How can we
minister to the Saviour's need?   Yet the answer comes,
" Inasmuch as ye did it unto the least of these My brethren,
ye have done it unto Me."[2]   Let us learn from Jesus to be
more feeling for others—less hard to others' needs—less deaf
to their appeal for aid.   Let us be Apostles of the Crucified
in these things.

> " O Love most patient, give me grace,
>   Make all my soul athirst for Thee ;
>   That parched, dry Lip, that fading Face,
>   That Thirst, were all for me."[3]

Again, this cry of Jesus was a confession of Human weakness.   This teaches us to follow His example.   In our
moments of weakness we are often nearer to God than when
we feel our own power and strength.   " Let him that
thinketh he standeth, take heed lest he fall."[4]   And doth
not this human weakness give us a special claim upon our
Father—our Saviour—our Sanctifier?   "We have no power
of ourselves to help ourselves."[5]   May we therefore so cast
our burden of weakness upon the Lord.

---

[1] " Daily Round," p. 143.   [2] S. Matt. xxv. 40.   [3] " Daily Round," p. 143.
[4] 1 Cor. ii. 12.   [5] Coll. II. Sun. in Lent.

The simplicity and childlike confidence of Jesus, too, is wonderfully shown in this Word of suffering. He had spoken of the children of His kingdom those mysterious words : " Blessed are they who do hunger and thirst after righteousness ; " [1] that is, to thirst to do the Father's Will, or as He again said, " My meat is to do the Will of Him that sent Me, and to finish His work." [2]

Our daily life should be framed after this model, for do not we each day pray, " Thy Will be done " ? Let us thirst for constant communion with our Heavenly Father. Let us thirst to do His Will. [3] " Thou wilt, O Blessed Jesus, that I should remain yet in this world of exile. Be it so ; but deign, O my God, favourably to answer my prayer. My soul sighs for Thee, thirsts for Thee : vouch-safe to have pity on me. Thou alone canst refresh me ; even Thou alone, my God."

THE FINISHED WORK.

I.

SIXTH WORD.

"It is finished."—S. JOHN XIX. 30.

RULY was Jesus " The Christ," The Anointed One, in His threefold office of King, Priest, and Prophet, so wonderfully portrayed in His glorious triumph of the Cross. " King," by virtue of His thorny crown : King proclaimed to mankind by testimony of His accusation—the title affixed to the Cross : King in

---

[1] S. Matt. v. 6.   [2] S. John iv. 34.
[3] Med. on " The Suffering Life of our Lord," p. 226.

H

His patient sufferings, in His noble and royal dignity of endurance during those dying hours of bitter pain and desolation : Priest in His one Sacrificial Act of Atonement for all sin: Priest and Victim, both combined in the mystery of His great Love, in which He willed to offer Himself on the Altar of the Cross as the true " Lamb of God," for lost mankind : Prophet, in those Seven Utterances revealing His very soul: that rich legacy of wisdom and love upon which we meditate to-day.

" It is finished."[1] Thus the Lord of Glory died—Thus the Royal Victor proclaimed the end to powers invisible and visible. It was no weak whisper like that cry of exhaustion, " I thirst." No! All His strength and power went forth in that mighty cry of triumph. The very powers of Hell were shaken, and Satan's dark angels shrouded their faces with fear at the voice of the dying God-Man.

" It is finished." The powers of evil are now undone : The penalty of sin is fully paid in the triumphant cry of the Conqueror :—The Father's will is perfected : The sinner's Ransom is completed. Oh! the mystery that surrounds the death of the Incarnate God. We cannot compass this until we learn the full extent of that Divine Love which led Him to such an awful sacrifice. Truly are we "*bought with a price*," my brothers—redeemed by Jesus' life-blood slowly ebbing away for our misdeeds.

> " For thee My Blood was shed,
>   For thee alone ;
>   I came to purchase thee
>   For My own."[2]

" It is finished." The end is proclaimed—the death-agony has set in, and Jesus has become " obedient unto death,

[1] S. John xvii. 30.   [2] Monro's " The Story of the Cross."

even the death of the Cross."[1] The pallid and blanched
Face worn by suffering tells of the last change. In a few
moments the pure Spirit of the Holy Jesus will have gone
to its rest. Six weary hours He had been hanging there
when the loud cry, " It is finished," was heard by hosts of
wondering angels in Heaven, and the Father knew that His
beloved Son had triumphed. All prophecy and type were
fulfilled. [2] " From friend and foe, from everyone on this
earth, He had received all that could be given, endured all
that could be endured ; and having fulfilled all that had to
be fulfilled, He had done all that was to be done."

Oh! glorious death-cry of my Saviour! May I ever remember this scene of Victory when tempted to give up the work
Thou hast appointed me. Let Thy blessed Passion and
Death be my help and support in times of weakness, my
guide and example when cast down, weary, and disconsolate,
to stir me up to new work and renewed acts of service for
Thee. Grant that this sacred scene may never be my condemnation. " Lord, what wouldest Thou have me to do?"[3]

Then comes the question, Why is my work so unfinished?
Why so imperfect? Why have I hitherto so failed in my
task? Because I do not *will* to follow Jesus to learn of
Him. Because His yoke hitherto hath been irksome to
me, and so my own burden of sin, slothful ease, and self-
will lies heavily upon me. Because I have neglected His
appointed means of grace. And so the Cross grows heavy,
and the way becomes weary, and the Evil One plies more
assiduously to keep my attention with his subtle temptings :
" No danger yet ; "—" Only this once ; "—" Everyone does
it ; "—" By-and-bye : "—as he endeavours to maim and cripple
me in my daily walk with God.

[1] Phil. ii. 8.   [2] Williamson's " Outstretched Hands," p. 47.   [3] Acts ix. 6

II.

"Looking unto Jesus, the Author and Finisher of our faith."
—HEB. XII. 2.

UR task may require us to make a keen, personal sacrifice, yet we must not shrink from it, or shirk it, or even do it in a half-hearted way, for though it be the dark valley of suffering we tread, and the steep hill of trial lies before us, yet that rocky pathway bears the imprint of the Saviour's feet, and it leads away from the world and evil—out of self—nearer and nearer to God.

We have not perfectly learned our lesson. "For Whom the Lord loveth, He chasteneth;"[1]—From those He loves best He takes most, or why those martyr death-beds of other days? Or again, Why this scene of Calvary? "It is enough for the disciple to be as his Master."[2]

"It is finished." Do not these words awaken within us sadder, sterner thoughts as we stand to behold His sufferings, and listen to His cry of victory. Our work will soon be ended—who can tell how soon—your work and mine? Will it be finished—perfected as Jesus' work was? Let each ask himself, Will the world, this parish, the little home circle of friends and relatives be the better for my living here? Have I left my mark for good upon God's world and God's people? Has my daily life been a silver thread to guide other souls onward and upward? My influence over human souls; what about that? If not all that is noble, and pure, and holy, let me start here, *as it were* at the foot of the Cross, not in my own strength, or after my own will, but let this blessed scene of grace and sadness teach the higher, better lesson, "Not my will, but

[1] Heb. xii. 6.   [2] S. Matt. x. 25.

Thine, O Lord," [1] and let me trust alone to His promise, " My grace is sufficient for thee." [2]

Oh! my brothers, let us " Draw nigh unto God, and He will draw nigh unto us." Nay, He will indeed draw us upward unto Himself, so that our Cross of suffering will be made glorious by the light of His presence, but " Our light affliction, which is but for a moment, worketh for us a far more exceeding and eternal weight of glory." [3]

" It is finished," again points me individually onward to the dark valley. " When the cold chills of death shall creep over me ; when the last family gathering shall assemble to exchange the loving farewells around my dying bed ; when the strong, clear voice shall be hushed ; when the tired arm shall lie helpless on the coverlet ; when the mist of the dark valley gathers around me, as the last commendatory prayers of the Church shall be read over me. " It is finished "—The life on earth, even as the shadows flee away, and the light of Paradise breaks upon the soul. Still the sobs of earth's beloved ones fall upon the ear, yet they have lost their sadness by mingling with angelic voices from that better land. " The silver cord is loosed," [4] and then shall all know the deep importance of the Saviour's triumph cry. Then shall we behold Him, Whom we have pierced, face to face, not by faith, and dimly shrouded by Calvary's gloom, but clearly, brightly, even as He is. Oh! happy death, which finishes such a life ! May God in His infinite mercy grant it to thee and me.

> " Lord, if Thou wilt, Make me Thine own,
> Give no companion, Save Thee alone ;
> Grant through each day of life To stand by Thee,
> With Thee when morning breaks, Ever with Thee." [5]

[1] S. Luke xxii. 42. [2] 2 Cor. xii. 9. [3] 2 Cor. iv. 17.
[4] Eccles. xii. 6. [5] Monro's " The Story of the Cross."

THE LIFE LAID DOWN.

I.

THE SEVENTH WORD.

" Father, into Thy Hands I commend My Spirit."—S. LUKE xxiii. 46.

EATH to the sinner is but the just reward for his evil deeds, but Death to the Sinless One must have been altogether abhorrent to His nature.

" It was a cruel rift in that pure life which never knew flaw," so Jesus cried to His Father in the words of the thirty-first Psalm—" Into Thy Hands I commend My Spirit." [1]

The mysterious darkness had melted away—a marvellous type of that deep, dark cloud of sin overshadowing lost mankind, now broken, dispelled, and passing away for ever before the bright beams of the Sun of Righteousness bringing Light and Life to all. Truly the Cross of Jesus—His Life—His Death—proclaim Him, "*The Light of the World.*"[2] May its pure rays enlighten thy life and mine! Yes, out of the bitter cloud of desolation and suffering beamed again the light of conscious communion with the Father, bringing the sweet balm of resignation to that weary One. Rest comes at length, and the tired Spirit flees to the Father's bosom.

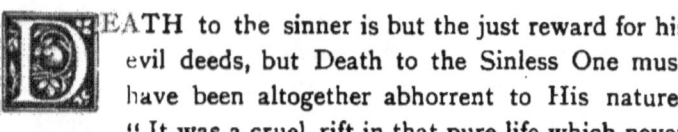

Thus the sweet story of Love and Sacrifice, so marvellously blended, begins and ends with the one word, "*Father*," showing [3] " The whole aim of His life, the whole thought of His soul to be His Father and His Father's Will." The last Word, as the first, begins with this. And, brothers, the Father of Jesus is our Father, and we too can begin, continue and end after this model of perfect obedience and

[1] Ps. xxxi. 6.   [2] S. John ix. 5.   [3] " The Mind of Jesus," p. 66.

filial confidence given by Him. [1] "God's Fatherliness is the one unfailing key to all the problems of life. Whatever comes close to us has living interest for Him."

Jesus not only teaches us "How to die!" but "How to live also!" by His last commendatory prayer from the Cross. The noblest lights, from the martyr spirit of Stephen down to the saintly efforts of men and women of to-day, have so framed their course—have so laid down their Cross beside the Divine Master's, breathing the same old prayer of faith and confidence.

Self-surrender is a beautiful ideal, yet it is a hard thing to accomplish. Men and women have sought this holy virtue in the calm peace of the cloister, thinking that apart from the world they might dwell the nearer to God. Others have sought it, and happily found it too, by ministering to the needs of suffering humanity, in the prison, the orphanage, the hospital, the battle-field, or the sick-chamber. Yet we need not go far out of the busy circle of daily life and work to find " *Our Father*," or even to give up " *Self*." He marks our motives, and pardons our shortcomings in our great struggle for the right. And Jesus the Divine Sufferer pleads for us too.

> " No earthly father loves like Thee,
>   No mother e'er so mild,
>   Bears and forbears as Thou hast done
>   With me, Thy sinful child." *Faber*.

The pathway to Heaven is now open to us. Our Elder Brother hath gone before to prepare a place for us. He reveals to us the Father with Outstretched Arms waiting for us, while He Himself is near to us to lead us onward. Death is but a journey Home, and the open door of Paradise

[1] Dr. Thorold, Bishop of Winchester.

reveals the face of Jesus to welcome us when the last brief struggle is over. We can willingly depart when His good pleasure calls us, if we have acted up to our motto, " Thou art my God : My times are in Thy Hand," [1] for the Father's Hand is the only quiet and secure place of rest.

II.

"Father, into Thy Hands I commend My Spirit."—S. LUKE XXIII. 46.

AN old Writer, S. Thomas à Kempis, teaches of God's Fatherliness :—" My son, forsake thyself, and thou shalt find Me—always, and at every hour ; as well in small things as in great. I expect nothing, but do desire that thou be found stripped of all things. Otherwise, how canst thou be Mine, and I thine, unless thou be stripped of all self-will, both within and without ? The sooner thou doest this, the better it will be with thee ; and the more fully and sincerely thou doest it, so much the more shalt thou please Me, and so much the greater shall be thy gain. Some there are who resign themselves, but with exceptions ; for they put not their whole trust in God, therefore they study how to provide for themselves. Some also at first do offer all, but afterwards, being assailed with temptation, they return again to their own ways, and therefore make no progress in the way of virtue. These shall not attain to the true liberty of a pure heart, nor to the favour of My sweetest friendship, unless they first make an entire resignation and a daily oblation of themselves. Without this, there neither is nor

[1] Ps. xxxi. 15.

can be a fruitful union. I have very often said unto thee,
and now again I say the same, 'Forsake thyself, resign
thyself, and thou shalt enjoy much inward peace. Give all
for all, seek nothing. Ask back nothing. Abide purely,
and with a firm confidence in Me, and thou shalt possess
Me; thou shalt be free in heart, and darkness shall not
tread thee down.' Let this be thy whole endeavour, let
this be thy prayer, this thy desire, that being stripped of
all selfishness, thou mayest with entire simplicity follow
Jesus only, and, dying to thyself, mayest live eternally
to Me."[1]

The gloom of Good Friday's sufferings will shortly break
to usher in the glorious Light of Easter joy, and victory.
May we who have watched and mourned around our dear
Master's Cross so die unto sin, that we may rise refreshed
to hail Him as our Risen Lord at His Festal Board on
Easter morning.

[2] "And here, brethren, we bring to an end our Lenten and
Good Friday Meditations. We have tried to penetrate a little
way *(how little a way God alone knows)* into the mysteries of our
dear Saviour's Passion and Sufferings." We have sought
for heart lessons to guide us in the future, to aid us in the
present, to blot out the evil of the past. We have all been
learners together at the foot of His Cross, as, " In Love
He suffered, in Love He died." Yes, brothers; your soul
and mine were present in His thoughts as He hung on
Calvary, and it was for you, and for me—as though there
were none other in this wide world—that He shed His
Blood, "and dying, resigned His weary Spirit into His
Father's keeping."

So let me die too in His arms.

[1] " The Imitation of Christ."   [2] " The Sinless Sufferer," p. 104.

For, " It is not darkness we are going to, for God is Light."

" It is not lonely, for Christ is with us."

" It is not an unknown country, for Christ is there." [1]

O SAVIOUR OF THE WORLD, WHO BY THY CROSS AND PRECIOUS BLOOD HAST REDEEMED US, SAVE US ; AND HELP US, WE HUMBLY BESEECH THEE, O LORD.

[1] C. Kingsley's words to his dying wife.

Additional.

I.

BURIED WITH JESUS.

Easter Eve.

"Now in the place where He was crucified there was a garden, and in the garden a new sepulchre, wherein was never man yet laid. There laid they Jesus."—S. JOHN XIX. 41.

HE watching by the Cross is now ended. The Passion has closed. The bruised and torn body of Jesus now sleeps peacefully. Sadness and stillness now reign through Jerusalem. The great price for man's Redemption has been fully paid as testified by the Victor's cry, "It is finished."[1] It is a time of restful hope for the true disciple as the gloom of Good Friday passes to herald in the brightness and glory of the Resurrection Morn.

What lessons have we learned beneath the Shadow of the Cross? Have we only been interested? Not moved with love or conviction? What then is our hope? It hath been said, "You may turn away from the Cross of Christ, but wherever you turn you will find, '*No more sacrifice for sins.*'"[2] "Behold," then, this "Lamb of God which taketh away the sin of the world."[3] Hath He not been "lifted up," and "evidently set forth crucified among you?"[4]

[1] S. John xix. 30.   [2] Heb. x. 26.   [3] S. John i. 29.
[4] Gal. iii. 1.

[1] "Other efforts of His power and love you may have resisted ; but there remains this highest—this last—the Love and Power of the Cross. Be your pilgrimage long or short, never pitch your tent but in sight of the Cross. More and more it will be to you the ' Pearl of great price,' [2] your Glory and the Crown of your rejoicing."

Jesus was buried. Loving hearts and tender hands prepared His lifeless body for the tomb. To minister to Him, their Beloved Lord and Master, even in death, was an act of love.

Calvary was now deserted—the Garden of the Sepulchre was now the place of interest. Thither wended the feet of those mournful watchers. How little did they understand His prophecy—" Destroy this Temple and in three days I will raise it up again." [3] The little band of holy Women, faithful to the last, Watchers at the Cross, are Watchers still at the Tomb, although it is guarded by the stern, harsh Roman Guards. Oh, how they loved Him ! Have we this love ? Our Faith may be brighter, our Hope is surer, but what about our Love ?

Then again, do we fear Death ? A modern Poet hath taught us to sing—

"Teach me to live, that I may dread
The grave as little as my bed ;
Teach me to die, that so I may
Rise glorious at the awful Day." [4]

May we therefore learn, as we contemplate the scene of Jesus buried, to regard the grave as a resting-place for this weak, tired-out body, when our work is finished—when our cross is laid down. May we learn so to die unto sin that

[1] " The Attraction of the Cross ; " Rel. Tract Soc.   [2] S. Matt. xiii. 46.
[3] S. Matt. xxvi. 61.   [4] John Keble.

by a continual mortifying of our corrupt affections we may
be buried with Jesus ; and that through the grave, and gate
of death, we may pass to our joyful resurrection.[1]

Yet how widely different was this pure lifeless Body to
all others sleeping in Death. "This Flesh saw no corruption,"[2] because there was sleeping the Sinless One,
" The Man of Sorrows," and yet " the Son of God."

Corruption cometh of sin. Jesus could not know it, for
the sins He had so nobly borne, and suffered for, were not
His own, but yours and mine. Do we understand this ?

Again, Paradise is opened to repentant souls. The rest
of God is proclaimed in Jesus. " There remaineth therefore a rest for the people of God. . . . . Let us labour
therefore to enter into rest,"[3] that " through the grave and
gate of death we may pass with Jesus to our joyful
Resurrection," for " rising from the dead implies life beyond
the grave," when our mourning shall be turned into joy,
and we shall receive " the garment of praise for the spirit
of heaviness."[4]

[1] Coll. for Easter Eve.   [2] Acts ii. 31.   [3] Heb. iv. 9-11.
        [4] Bp. Thorold, " Questions of Faith and Duty."

II.

THE RISEN LIFE.

EASTER DAY.

"Because I live, ye shall live also."—S. JOHN XIV. 19.

HAT a wonderful time is this! How mysteries follow closely upon each other! One after another of God's mighty secrets are revealed to us! But two days ago that God in Jesus should die! To-day, that a dead man, even Jesus, should raise Himself, and live for ever as the Conqueror of Death and Sin.

The Sepulchre is empty. The Resurrection Story hath been told by Angel lips to the sorrowing women who drew near to the Tomb. The pure soul of the Divine Sufferer has returned from the Unseen World. The Glorified Body of the Lord again appears to His chosen ones, the Disciples.

Truly, "This is the day which the Lord hath made, we will rejoice and be glad in it."[1]

No human hands unsealed the empty tomb! No band of warriors were needed to overpower the Roman Watch, for "The Angel of the Lord descended from Heaven, and came, and rolled back the stone from the door,"[2] to reveal to Redeemed Mankind the truth of the Resurrection—

"Jesus Christ hath risen to-day, Alleluia!"[3]

Man saw Him die. Man watched His sufferings on Calvary's tree.

None beheld His Moment of Glory and Victory as the

[1] Ps. cxviii. 24 (*P. B. Version*).   [2] S. Matt. xxviii. 2.   [3] Easter Hymn.

Risen Lord. What a rush of Alleluias fills the courts of Heaven, while earthly choirs rejoice to blend their anthem strains with the Angel hosts.

> " The strife is o'er, the battle done ;
> The triumph of the Lord is won ;
> O let the song of praise be sung.
> Alleluia ! " *Easter Hymn.*

At Eastertide there is a general Resurrection. Nature arises from her winter's sleep ; buds, and birds, and bees, and flowers, all unconsciously teach the Resurrection Truth. Shall not we arise ? What is the outcome of our Lenten watchings ? Have we not learnt there, " Apart with Jesus," the true nature of evil ! and what sin hath done to our God ! Have we not buried the old sins—natures—habits with Him ? Therefore may we arise to-day with holy vigour to live the new life in Him. The Angel's message proclaims that— Sin hath been rolled away—the fear of death hath been rolled away—misery and eternal separation hath been rolled away by our Jesus.

The Resurrection was not merely a fact in the history of the world. It was this, but far more—to you—to me—to our souls. It was a reality, whereby we gained freedom, joy, victory, salvation, and Life Eternal. " Because I live, ye shall live also."[1] Sin and its penalties were rolled away at the Resurrection. There was commenced the opening of the purer life of victory. Look at lost mankind before the Sacrifice of Jesus for the sin of the whole world ! Every act of sin made the gulf deeper, the sea wider to separate man from God. Now sin gives place to pardon, peace, and victory by and through Jesus. Dark fear hath given place

[1] S. John xiv. 19.

to bright hope, for death in Jesus is the Gate of Life—The Beginning, not the End.

See the power of the Resurrection in the death scene of the first Martyr, Stephen—"Lord Jesus, receive my spirit,"[1] or in the cry of the faltering disciple, Thomas, "My Lord and my God."[2]

May not this Resurrection Day of Jesus point us onward to another Resurrection Day of the Lord, when all will be finally rolled away which separates us from God—when the choirs of earth shall sing with angel hosts the Triumph Song of victory and joy—when Eastertide will be kept by adoring souls around the Throne of God.

" By Thy glorious Resurrection, Good Lord, deliver us." *Amen.*

[1] Acts vii. 59.   [2] S. John xx. 28.

A HARMONY OF OUR BLESSED LORD'S PASSION.

TIME.	RECORD OF EVENTS.	S. MATTHEW	S. MARK.	S. LUKE.	S. JOHN.
PALM SUNDAY.	Christ enters Jerusalem—weeps over city	xxi. 1.	xi. 1.	xix. 29 41.	xii. 2.
	Visit of the Greeks, etc.				,, 20.
MONDAY.	Cursing the fig tree	,, 18.	,, 12.		
	Cleansing the Temple	,, 12.	,, 15.	,, 45.	
	Return to Bethany	,, 17.	,, 19.		
TUESDAY.	Fig tree withered	,, 20.	,, 20.		
	Jesus in the Temple teaching	,, 23 ; xxiv. 1.	, 27 ; xiii. 1.	xx. 1 ; xxi. 5.	
	Teaching on the Mount of Olives	,, 3 ; xxv. 31.	,, 3.	,, 7.	
WEDNESDAY.	Plotting of chief priests with Judas	xxvi. 3-14.	xiv. 1-10.	xxii. 1-3.	
THURSDAY.	The Passover	,, 17-20.	,, 12-17.	,, 7-14.	xiii. 1.
	The Lord's Supper	,, 26.	,, 22.	,, 19.	
	Discourses with the Disciples				xiv. 1.
	The way to Gethsemane	,, 30.	,, 26.		,, 17.
	Christ's Agony in the Garden	,, 36-40.	,, 32-37.	,, 39-43.	xviii. 1.
GOOD FRIDAY.	The Betrayal	,, 47.	,, 43.	,, 47.	,, 3.
	Trial before Annas and Caiaphas	,, 57.	,, 53.	,. 54.	,, 13.
	The Denial of S. Peter	,, 58.	,, 54.	,, 55.	,, 15.
	The Trial before Pilate	xxvii. 1-27.	xv. 1-16.	xxiii. 1-23.	,, 28. xix. 16.
	The way to Calvary	,, 82.	,, 21.	,, 26.	
	The Crucifixion	,, 34-51.	,, 23-37.	,, 83-46.	,, 17-31.
GOOD FRIDAY EVENING.	The Burial by Joseph of Arimathæa	,, 57-60.	,, 42-46.	,, 50-52.	,, 38-40.
EASTER DAY.	The Resurrection and Appearances during the Great Forty Days	xxviii. 20.	xvi. 1-18.	xxiv. 1-49.	xx. 1 ; xxi. 24.
ASCENSION DAY.	The Ascension (see also Acts i. 9-12)		,, 19, 20.	,, 50-53.	

THE SEVEN WORDS FROM THE CROSS.

No.		S. MATTHEW	S. MARK.	S. LUKE.	S. JOHN.
I.	"Father, forgive them !"			xxiii. 34.	
II.	"To-day shalt thou be."			,, 43.	
III.	"Woman, behold thy son."				xix. 25-27.
IV.	"My God ! My God !"	xxvii. 45.	xv. 33.		
V.	"I thirst."				,, 28.
VI.	"It is finished."				,, 30.
VII.	"Father, into Thy hands."		,, 50.	,, 37.	,, 46.

I

✝

Glory

be

to the Father,

and to the Son :

and to the Holy Ghost ;

As it was

in the Beginning,

is now,

and ever shall be :

world without end.

Amen.

www.ingramcontent.com/pod-product-compliance
Lightning Source LLC
Chambersburg PA
CBHW020747020726
47495CB00008B/2341